It was exactly t
when big Fergu
window of the
high-rise tower
second before, Byron realized that going up there had been the worst idea he'd had for a very long time, but by then it was too late.

The trouble was that after a year in the Scrubs Byron thought he was hard. Bugger it, he knew he was hard, because nobody you met in there took your word for it. You had to prove it once or twice before a man would move round you, and he could look back with some satisfaction on the fact that no one had got up his nose without getting a kicking. The last occasion being the time he'd knocked the shit out of a punchy ex-boxer in the showers.

Byron didn't realize what was happening until he felt the cold wind on his face, and then he screamed and began clinging to the window-sill with his fingers, but the pressure urging him out was irresistible, and in another instant, almost too fast for thought, he was falling.

FAST ROAD TO NOWHERE

JOE CANZIUS

VISTA

First published in Great Britain 1996
as a Vista paperback original

Vista is an imprint of the Cassell Group
Wellington House, 125 Strand, London WC2R 0BB

A catalogue record for this book is
available from the British Library

ISBN 0 575 60104 3

Typeset by CentraCet Ltd, Cambridge
Printed and bound in Great Britain
by Cox & Wyman Ltd, Reading, Berks

96 97 98 99 10 9 8 7 6 5 4 3 2 1

For Jenny, without whom it would have been impossible, and for my grandad Joe, whose art was his life, and whose life was the first story I understood.

Thanks to Laurie, who put the idea in my head, and to Barry and Fred, all of them special bookies, and a good laugh too.

Chapter 1

It was exactly three thirty-seven in the afternoon when big Fergus threw Byron Desire through the window of the flat on the twentieth floor of the high-rise tower on the estate in Hulme. A split second before, Byron realized that going up there had been the worst idea he'd had for a very long time, but by then it was too late.

The trouble was that after a year in the Scrubs Byron thought he was hard. Bugger it, he knew he was hard, because nobody you met in there just took your word for it. You had to prove it once or twice before a man would move round you, and although he hadn't done anything to mess up his chances of an early parole over the last six months he could look back with some satisfaction on the fact that no one had got up his nose without getting a kicking. The last occasion being the time when he'd knocked the shit out of a punchy ex-boxer in the showers. That had been some time before Christmas. The guy had just been moved from Brixton, where, Byron heard later, he'd been a bit of a face. Of course Byron would have been more circumspect, boxed a bit clever, if his mates hadn't been standing round, but by then he was well in with the rest of the black mafia in the Scrubs, and there was no way he could let a white inmate, no matter how bad he was, touch up his arse without giving him a good slap. After that Byron had not been obliged to exert himself again. But, bugger it, he *knew* he was well hard.

The trouble was that he'd forgotten about geezers like Fergus. He hadn't even been thinking about geezers like Fergus. He'd come straight up on the train from London after he got out, because he couldn't think of what else to do. After all, when Byron had been arrested he was stopping in the same flat in Hulme with his girlfriend Marie, and he thought of it as home. The baby Hyacinth had been nearly a year old then and Byron was looking forward to seeing both of them as much as he had ever looked forward to anything. Not that he felt that much about Marie. When her letters had stopped a couple of months into his stretch he hadn't worried a lot. For a start they were never much longer than a page and only contained boring bits of information about what her mother, her auntie and her best friend were doing that week, which mostly consisted of going to the shop and having arguments at the dole office. Byron didn't need it, as he told himself, especially when she managed to misspell even the simplest words. One day he'd spent close on half an hour trying to figure out what she meant by 'bassterred'.

But he wasn't worried when he got off the train at Piccadilly. If anyone had been looking at Byron what they would have seen was a tall good-looking brownskin boy about twenty with his hair done in a cute fade and smooth features, who looked as if he didn't have a care in the world. He was wearing jeans, a T-shirt and an old bomber jacket which still looked good, and he walked with a slight swagger, slinging his bag over his shoulder and stepping off down the platform, hurrying to catch up with the girl he'd been talking to in the corridor outside the toilet. He hadn't got a seat. The trains seemed a lot more crowded than they used to be, and even the odd empty seat was reserved, so he'd ended up by the window in between cars. The girl had come running along the platform, and he'd grabbed her bag from her and swung it up, then helped her in just as the train was starting to move. She had been red and panting and for a moment Byron had a mad desire to grab her and push her up against the door right there and then. He hadn't been this close to a woman for such a long time, for more than a year, and the situation was like a continuation of the fantasies he had lying in his bunk late at night stroking his raging and irrepressible dick.

The girl fitted well in his fantasies too. She was tall with shoulder-length black hair and greyish green eyes which wavered a little at the beginning then stared steadily at him. Her complexion was very pale and she had wide full lips. But it was her big firm curving breasts which held Byron's attention. When he'd first noticed them as she got in the train he'd tried to look away, but something about them kept dragging his attention back. It was like the time he'd gone to Madame Tussaud's with the other kids in his foster home. He'd walked past the sleeping princess without looking, because at nine years old he'd despised all that weepy girl's fairy-tale balls, but somehow he'd known that something was going on behind him, and the hair had climbed upright on the back of his neck, till he turned round and nearly jumped out of his skin when he saw her breathing. It was the same with this girl's tits. He just had to look. He could have sworn she was thrusting them right in his face and he thought of the words in which he would describe her to one of his cellmates, Biggy, a Jamaican a few years older than himself. Biggy had a reputation for being hard. He was doing life and a degree with the Open University, but what he really liked to talk about was women, their tits and their pussies and what he used to do when he had access to them; and he had some mad tales, like the one about the woman writer who used to come in to lecture to the literature class, dressed in a tight sweater and a micro-skirt and her legs spread so he could see her crotch while he jerked off under cover of the desk. Byron didn't know whether or not he believed it, but the way Biggy told it was one of the funniest things he'd heard before or since. Eyeing up the girl's tits, he began framing the words in which he'd tell Biggy about all this, and then it struck Byron that talking to Biggy was a habit he would have to lose, because with any luck they would never meet again.

The girl must have noticed Byron staring, because she turned away a little, and Byron raised his gaze hurriedly, curving his lips in a polite smile. The trouble was that from the moment he saw her he'd developed a permanent erection which continued to nudge the front of his jeans all the way through the trip. He suspected that she noticed. He couldn't be sure, because although she'd been a bit stiff and short with him at first, he thought that might have been because he was black. Well, he thought, not black, mixed race. He'd got out of the habit of thinking of himself as mixed in the Scrubs because the brothers didn't deal with no mixtures. You were black or you were nothing. But he guessed that all these fine distinctions wouldn't make much difference to the girl anyway. Without thinking about it or even rehearsing the story in his mind he told her that he was finding everything a bit strange because he had been travelling abroad and this was the end of his time off. Now he was about to enter Manchester University. After that the girl loosened up, while Byron felt a quiet sense of triumph at having pressed the right button. He'd got this university story from a dealer he'd shared a cell with for a few weeks, and he'd guessed that a class chick like this one would go for it. He wasn't worried about how to sound like a student because he'd listened carefully to some of the brothers who were doing Open University classes, and he knew what to say. A few words like 'deconstruction', and he'd be laughing, Biggy had said, letting him into the secret. Nobody understood what the bloody hell all that was about, he said, only none of them would admit it. Just go on, say them words, you'll see.

But, as it happened, he didn't have to talk much. When the girl relaxed she took off on a long recital of her life and times. Her name was Katrina and by coincidence, she said, she was a student. Her boyfriend was a student too, some kind of acting student, and she went on about all the clubs they frequented, while Byron mimed and mugged surprise, delight, and polite interest, acting out reactions he hadn't used, or had any use for, over the last couple of years. For an hour or so Byron felt like an actor, playing to a gullible audience, and he loved it.

On the platform he took her telephone number and arranged to take her for a drink, then watched the wiggle that her beautiful behind was giving him as she strode firmly out of the station.

'Oh, Jesus,' Byron muttered to himself. 'Oh, what I could do with that.'

He began thinking about how he'd get on to her when they met for a drink. She'd be dead easy, he thought. A few bevvies and it wouldn't be hard to get his hand into her knickers and then he imagined himself on top of her and groaned aloud again. But first he'd have to sus out somewhere they could go. He couldn't take her back to the flat. She lived with her parents, she'd told him, and unless she was prepared to go down one of the empty bays down the flats with him it was goodnight campers. But somehow she didn't look the kind of girl who it would be easy to talk into going up against the wall.

The problem occupied him all the way down to Moss Side, and it wasn't until he was walking down Moss Lane East that Byron started thinking about Marie again. Byron had met her down a shebeen off Princess Road a week after he'd arrived from Barnsley, but she was still at school, and when she got pregnant she'd left without bothering to take her exams. Her mum, a Jamaican lady who'd moved up from Birmingham and still talked through her nose the way they did there, made a lot of noise, but Marie had four sisters and Byron had the feeling that her mum was not completely displeased at the prospect of her youngest getting out of the crowded flat in Cheadle Hulme to settle down with a boy who at least didn't seem to object to taking care of his responsibilities. He hadn't had to deal with her dad because he'd disappeared years ago, and Marie didn't remember anything about him anyway.

The lift was working, although it still smelt of urine and dog shit. By the time it arrived and the grimy doors slid open, there was a little family standing behind Byron, waiting to join him for the ride. The mother was a monstrously fat white woman with greasy turd-coloured hair hanging round her face in sticky strands, escorted by a boy and a girl who looked to be twins, about ten years old, dirty yellow hair, rat-like features, leather jackets with metal studs stuck all over them, and shiny little tin guitars pinned in front. Each one was leading a Doberman by a short leash. Byron looked at the kids and the dogs looked back at him, salivating. Byron figured that this was how they looked at fresh meat, so he clutched his bag in front of his privates and stepped into the corner of the lift as far as possible from the group. They got off at the tenth floor, and walked away without a word, but the dogs had kept their eyes fixed on him all the time, and as they got out one of them looked back at him as if weighing up an opportunity that he'd missed.

Byron went on up to the twentieth. He could feel the cold wind whistling along the walkways. Spring was nearly over, and in the train he'd seen green things growing all along the railway tracks. But up here in the flats the walkways made a tunnel along which rushed an icy blast carrying slivers of cold water, flinging the stinging droplets into his face as soon as he stepped out of the lift.

Byron had stopped in front of two-fifty-seven, a blue

door same as he remembered it, and knocked. The bell had never worked. A man opened the door.

'Who are you?' Byron asked.

It wasn't the coolest opening line but Byron had been taken by surprise, and at the back of his mind was the thought that this might be a cousin or brother or other relative that he hadn't heard about. So he was kind of expecting recognition, then an explanation, and maybe Marie running out from the back to throw her arms round him. Something like that. But that wasn't the way it went.

For a start the guy's expression didn't change. Not at all; and the expression on his face was one that Byron recognized only too well, a cold hard stare, the eyes level in an immobile mask of a face, which still managed to give the impression of boiling rage within. Byron hadn't been prepared but habit asserted itself in a flash and he gave the guy the same hard stare right back.

'Who the fuck you is?' the guy said in his turn.

The thought crossed Byron's mind that maybe Marie had moved.

'Marie don't live here no more?' he said, moderating his look by the smallest fraction.

For a moment the guy didn't reply. Instead he stared steadily down at Byron, sizing him up. The Doberman in the lift flashed through Byron's mind, and he narrowed his eyes. Unfortunately he was looking up, because this guy was at least four, maybe five, maybe even six inches taller. He was broad too, nearly filling the door with his shoulders. From the top of his head rasta locks descended like angry black snakes coiling over his shoulders, and the scar which ran down the side of his face seemed to be swelling and pulsing as Byron looked at it. Byron had seen many bad black men during his time inside, and before, but this was one of the baddest he had ever seen.

'Marie live here, yes,' the giant said, 'but them gone see her mudda right now.'

Byron considered for a moment. He didn't want to tangle with this geezer, but, bugger it, this was his house, his child, and as far as he was concerned, his woman too. He had a right, he thought, and a slow burn began somewhere inside his guts.

'So wha go on?' Byron said, the dialect coming to his lips naturally. He had begun speaking in imitation of the rude boys years ago when he first arrived in Moss Side, and the time he'd spent in the Scrubs had made him word perfect. 'Ah my baby dat y'know, Hyacinth.'

'You Byron?' the giant asked.

'Right,' Byron said. 'That's me.'

That was his second mistake. The first, he already knew, had been coming up here without finding out what was going on in Marie's life.

'So who are you?' Byron continued.

'I live here now,' the giant said simply.

Byron thought about his options. He could piss off and disappear, forget about the whole thing. He could wait down by the lift till Marie came back, or he could kick the giant in the balls, punch him down and kick him some more.

As if reading his mind the giant smiled.

'Come in nuh, man?' he said. 'We have to talk.'

Byron blinked. This was the last thing he expected but a few minutes later he was sitting in the front room of the flat, looking round at the room where he'd spent so much of his time sat with Marie and Hyacinth, watching the football on telly. During the match when Maradona had touched the ball in, he'd gone half-way round the bend and if the Argy had been in the room that time he'd have shown him a thing or two about the use of hands. If the room had any kind of memory, it wouldn't have forgotten, because the way he'd screamed and shouted must be branded in its walls. He cast his eyes about, as if checking for a welcoming sign, but there was nothing. Even his photos had gone from the top of the telly, and he thought grimly about what he'd have to say to Marie when she came back.

The giant's name was Fergus, and now Byron was inside the room he seemed to loosen up, even his accent seemed to have softened and got less hard and jerky.

'Listen to me, boss,' Fergus said. 'Me din know nothin bout you when I move in here. Y'understand?'

Byron nodded stiffly.

'All right. I like Marie y'know, and the little girl too. I can see your position. It's tough, a man inside and him don't know wha go on. Him come out and another man take over. Feel bad bout dat, y'know.'

Byron could hardly believe his ears. Fergus was apologizing. It was right then that he made his third mistake. Later on, thinking back, it struck him that the problem was that he still hadn't got it into his head that the life he'd been leading while banged up was abnormal. Behind bars there were certain truths every bad boy held to be eternal. Might is right. Do the bastards before they do you. Being strong means never having to say sorry. The fact that Fergus was apologizing meant that, big and bad as he looked, the giant was worried, or even scared about what he might do about the theft of his woman and his daughter.

Byron's reaction was automatic. He'd been holding back the burn inside his belly, and now he let the brakes off and felt it gradually start to grow into a warm tickling that he knew would slowly mount right through his chest into his brain.

'Feeling bad don't help me,' he said brusquely.

Fergus spread his hands, apologetic again.

'I know that,' he said. 'Maybe best if you come back

later, y'know. Talk with her and see how the runnings go.'

Now Byron was sure. Under all those muscles the guy was really a big pussy and he was about to back down. He wasn't at all certain what he wanted out of the situation but he knew that once he'd asserted that he was the dominant personality, anything could happen.

'Don't tell me bout no runnings,' he shouted. 'This is my flat, and I'm back.'

He felt pretty good saying that, and he watched Fergus closely to see what the effect was. The little red eyes watched him back steadily, and a little spark of doubt winked across Byron's brain.

'Me don't wan talk bout this no more,' Fergus said slowly. 'Me try fah reason with you. But this my flat now, you no see? I think you better go.'

On the last words Fergus said, his accent had suddenly disappeared and he'd started speaking in straightforward Mancunian. As if in reaction Byron had found himself replying in the voice of his native Yorkshire.

'Wait a minute,' he said.

'Listen, dickhead,' Fergus told him, paying no attention. 'I want you out.'

He pointed his forefinger angrily in Byron's face and Byron slapped it aside automatically. This was Byron's final error. Fergus stared at him for a moment, his eyes seeming to go smaller and redder. Then he began unfolding his bulk from the chair. Byron knew better than to wait for another cue. He had to get the first blow in, and he moved without thinking, getting his fast hands on the legs of a wooden cocktail table, and heaving it round, the copies of *Pride*, *The Voice*, the *Sun* and an old GUS catalogue flying past him, together with a couple of mugs spraying a sprinkling of stale coffee. He didn't know where they went because in the time it took him to register their passage the table was smashing full into

Fergus's massive shoulders. Byron was aiming for his head and the giant must have pulled it out of the way in time, but he went over with a satisfying crash. Still he didn't seem to be stunned or even hurt, because he started getting up immediately. The table had disintegrated, leaving Byron holding two short legs, and although he contemplated going after Fergus with them, his next thought was to make a run for it and get the hell out of the door. But it was too late. Fergus was up and facing him, a look of animal rage twisting his features into a terrifying mask. Byron took off, trying to swerve round him, but as he did so the giant's hands fastened on the back of his jacket and pulled him back with a frighteningly inexorable pressure.

Byron didn't remember too much about the next bit. He remembered struggling with Fergus, and he'd brought his knee up between the thick legs, but the guy had twisted so that the blow was cushioned by his thighs. Either that or he had iron bollocks, because he hadn't doubled up in pain or reacted in any other way, except to begin half dragging, half carrying Byron across the room, ignoring the increasingly frantic blows that were being hammered into his ribs.

Byron didn't realize what was happening until he felt the cold wind on his face, and then he screamed and began clinging to the window-sill with his fingers, but the pressure urging him out was irresistible, and in another instant, almost too fast for thought, he was falling.

It was only later on, when he woke from bad dreams in the dark of night, that Byron remembered the sheer terror he felt as he went out of the window. At the moment he fell what he was trying to do was pray, but all he could think of was the word 'god', then 'mum', and these words filled his head, so that he couldn't be sure whether or not he'd actually been shouting them. But just before the incredible impact blacked out his world he thought that putting his mum and god together was probably right, because he'd never seen either of them, and he couldn't be sure that they existed, and even if they did, he was willing to bet that neither of them gave a shit about him.

Chapter 2

When Sonia read about what had happened to Byron in the paper, her first instinct was to ring the hospital right away. But since it was only half-past six in the morning and Charlie and her friend Vange were already installed in the office, sorting out the rota for the day, she reckoned she would wait till she could find an unattended phone somewhere else.

'You ready then, my darling?' Charlie said in the tone of fake sweetness that she used towards Sonia, and towards the other women on the job whom she fancied. Sonia nodded and gave her a smile, but she wasn't fooled. She'd seen Charlie turn into a raving bitch too often to imagine that the sugar and spice would last beyond Charlie getting what she wanted, and, even before her courtships had run their course, Charlie could turn very nasty if you came in late or anything else went wrong. In fact there was something about both Charlie and Vange which gave Sonia the creeps. Part of it was the way they looked. Both of them must have been close to six feet tall, towering above Sonia, who didn't think of herself as a small girl anyway. The physical similarity ended there because Vange was thin and cadaverous with a gaunt haggard face, big nose and big horse teeth which were always bared in an anxious grin which had nothing to do with humour. In contrast Charlie was big and blocky with a chest and shoulders which wouldn't have looked out of place on one of the wrestlers you saw on TV, the Mighty Hulk the girls called her behind her back. In front of her she carried a fat stomach which bulged out the top of her jeans so that her big leather belt looked like the hoop round a barrel, and she had big square hands and a broad square grim face, which made it all the more alarming when she gave you one of her long slow smiles, her muddy brown eyes fixed and staring urgently, the appeal in them inescapable and somehow terrifying.

Vange's manner couldn't have been more different. She wore long flowered dresses which flapped around her thin calves and her thick greying brown hair was always brushed out in a sort of fine mop sticking out over her shoulders, her scrawny neck bearing the whole thing up, and twitching convulsively from time to time like some kind of zonked out and decadent pre-Raphaelite chicken, while her watery grey eyes slid past you, so you could never quite tell where she was looking.

Every morning, while the job lasted, this pair would be the first thing that Sonia saw. Vange drooping around next to Charlie who'd be bent over her paperwork togged out in her usual motorcycle boots, jeans and a black leather jacket crusted with zips, stars and badges. On the mornings when Sonia was hungover or still speeded up on E or whatever she'd been given or bought the night before, she used to close her eyes and shake her head as if trying to rouse herself from a bad dream. But she also knew that all this really was like a kind of nightmare from which she wouldn't wake up until she'd brought her load back and checked out for the afternoon.

On the day that Sonia saw the story about Byron's accident Charlie and Vange weren't in the best of moods. One of the women they'd been expecting that day had dropped out, and they were going to have to contact the job centre and get another one in a hurry. This was always happening.

'I dunno what they bleeding want,' Charlie roared, and Vange made a squeaking noise which signified agreement.

'And they reckon the unemployment figures are going up all the time. I dunno.'

I'd like to see you doing it, Sonia thought viciously as she grabbed her list of pick-ups out of Charlie's hand and clattered off down the stairs. As she walked across the floor of the depot towards the yard where the vans were kept, closing her mind off from the smell, she wondered also when she'd be able to get out of this herself. Nobody ever stayed any longer than they could help. The job was frigging messy, filthy, demanding, and on top of that, left you feeling as if the stink was invading your pores and settling round you like a cloud. Bad enough but the cloud got right into your mind as well. After only a couple of weeks she couldn't bear to tell people just what it was she did, even though it was a women-only job, and when she'd heard about it at the Job Centre she'd thought, hello, good one.

Sonia started the van, slid the window open as usual and drove off. This was the last time for the rest of the day when she would feel more or less normal, and she liked to enjoy zipping along through South London up through Clapham towards the river, in and out of the early morning traffic breathing good air for the last time. On the way she thought about Byron. She'd heard, in a roundabout way, that he'd had some trouble and been banged up but she didn't know how or why, and at the time she hadn't had the space or the energy to spare for finding out what was going on. But that morning, as she focused on the words in the paper, a pang like an electric shock, the sort you got from sticking your finger in the light socket by mistake, that kind of pang, had run through her whole body when she read Byron's name in the report about the man who'd gone out of the twentieth-floor window of the flats in Manchester. She guessed that was because Byron was the nearest thing to a brother that she had. She felt about the same kind of attachment to Willie, but Willie was younger and it was different. She'd always looked up to Byron, and when the time had come for him to be released from the care of the council, and to leave the foster-home where they were all living, Sonia had cried and cried, quietly to herself at night, so that nobody heard. She thought of it as a long time ago, but remembering those days was enough to bring the tears springing behind her eyes.

So, although she'd been sort of resigned to losing touch with Byron, she still had a fantasy of them getting together again, with her all tall and grown up, maybe with somebody really nice next to her, and, 'This is my brother,' she would have said, and maybe Byron would give her a secret smile and introduce her to everyone as his sister. They very nearly were, to her way of thinking, because it couldn't be just a coincidence that they'd all ended up together in the same house, five mixed-race kids, and all the kids they ran into assumed that they were brothers and sisters. Half-caste, they used to call them, and she'd always hated that expression. But out of the other four Byron had been the one she was closest to, and he was the one who had looked after her, even though he was a couple of years older and definitely a tasty-looking geezer and all the girls at the schools they went to fancied him to death.

These memories were occupying Sonia's mind to such an extent that she'd stopped worrying about her own troubles, like whether she'd ever manage to find another flat before they evicted her from the squat, or whether Mrs Holland would take the trouble to keep her hand on Juliet's pushchair all the time she was out; and it seemed only a few minutes before she was driving into the forecourt of the first building she was due to visit. She walked right in without speaking to anyone, the way she usually did. It was a government building, and she supposed there was some sort of security system but the doorman knew her well enough by now, nineteen-year-old pale brown girl, curly brown mane, every day the same boots and jeans and a sweater with rolled up sleeves, gloves on her hands, walking in and carrying the bundles of boxes a little awkwardly, so that from behind it looked like she was giving him a slow wriggle showing off her arse all the way up the corridor. No one challenged her any more as she walked in, except that the doorman, old Joss, gave her his dirty grin and a 'Hello, love'.

It was a big building with about ten floors, two ladies' toilets on each floor and a couple of extra ones up on the ninth and tenth. That was where the bosses hung out, and as Joss put it to her one day, they had to have extra loos because they were more full of wind and piss than anyone else in the building. She wouldn't know about that, she replied, because she hardly ever saw them except once or twice, tall paunchy guys in pinstripes, and carefully groomed women in dark suits and high heels who looked at her without a smile, their eyes blankly contemptuous, as if she was part of the sanitary arrangements, which she supposed she was. On the other hand, she thought, she was young and slim, she got all the exercise she needed for free, and she had a nice body with good tits even if she said so herself, and it would be a long time before she had to stick perfume bottles between her legs, so suck that you haggard old bitches.

She had a system. She'd bring in enough boxes to fix the loos on each floor. Sometimes she'd do two at a time. It wasn't complicated. All she did was go into the loo, lift the container which held the used tampons and napkins from its holder, put in on the floor beside her, and slide an empty one in. Then she would take the container down the corridor to the next loo, do it all over again, and walk out holding the two full boxes back to the van. She described it once to Mrs Holland when she went to drop off Juliet in the morning and when you said it that way it sounded dead easy and probably the first one or two floors were not so bad. You came out thinking what were you so worried about all the way up from Clapham, guts twisting and churning and trying not to feel sick about the day ahead. But by the time she'd cleared the third or fourth floor she was into the full misery of it, moving automatically, tensing her arms round the warm smooth sides of the containers, turning her head away, trying not to smell the rotting stink of the women's waste inside. It wasn't the weight so much, although that was bad enough. Arnold Schwarzenegger should try this lot for a change, she used to mutter to herself. Strength and endurance. No man could take the pace. Sometimes she used to time herself, trying to set up records which she could break the next day or the day after. The trouble was she always forgot her times and was reduced to guessing whether she was better at it, or whether it was getting to her and slowing her down into the kind of zombie who'd been doing the job for months and months, a permanent sneer twisted into her face, as if there was a bad smell under her nose all the time, which after a while, at least in your mind, there certainly was.

An hour later Sonia was on the top floor. It was round about eight and some people had begun to come in. She could hear the echoes drifting up from the lower floors and as she went up in the lift some cleaners came in after her, two depressed-looking Pakistani women with mops and buckets and a surly young African geezer carrying keys. But the upper floors where she was now were deserted, and she guessed the kind of people who worked upstairs wouldn't be coming in for another couple of hours, so after she'd cleared the loos, she set her containers down and went to the nearest phone.

She got the hospital easily enough but when she asked about Byron the woman on the phone didn't seem to know and she wouldn't tell her anything useful. After a while Sonia persuaded her to take a message. She said it was urgent because she was his little sister, his only relative in the world, and in the message she left her name and telephone number, hoping that the woman on the other end was writing it down like she said she was. After that she hung up, but by then two men had come in and seen her with the receiver in her hand. They were both boss types, one of them older, with smooth blond hair slicked back and sharp staring deep-set eyes. The other one was younger, dark-haired with a smooth-skinned fatty look about him. They didn't say anything to her and she hurried to pick up her boxes and scurry out, before they could work out what to do about one of the skivvies picking up the phone and breathing into it. But they caught up with her at the lift, and to her surprise the tall one with the sharp eyes gave her a big smile. Her surprise wasn't exactly agreeable, because she sussed right away that the smile he was giving her had something leering and strangely proprietorial about it as if he thought he owned her, or at least owned the piece of her he was interested in.

'Morning,' he boomed at her. This sort of man always talked loud like this, as if he didn't give a shit who heard him. Sonia ducked her head in reply and went into the lift in front of them clutching her boxes. That was when she felt a hand on her hip. It wasn't particularly intrusive or suggestive. It didn't squeeze or pinch or tickle or move a stiff finger around anything sensitive, but it was there. Sonia looked round. Blondie was watching her with a sort of calculating smile. Sonia knew what that meant, because by now she knew that guys like this thought a girl who carried the crap up and down every morning was probably game for anything and would be grateful too. In other circumstances, she had to admit that this geezer, ancient as he was, could probably pull them, her too, if she had a few glasses of gin inside her and nothing else on that night. But there was something about the way he flicked his eyes sideways at his young companion which pissed her off. Probably, she thought, if she'd been the African boy or one of the tired Pakistani ladies he'd have looked straight over her head at the wall, the way they did sometimes, ignoring your existence. But, as she knew only too well, a stiff dick has no prejudices, or very few anyway. Depending on the circumstances, that is.

'You're bright and early, little lady,' Blondie uttered, giving her that same foxy little smile. 'What's that you've got there?' He pointed at the boxes.

Sonia had no idea why she did what she did then, because she didn't give a damn really, she could have smiled at him or given him a harmless answer or just paid no attention. She might have done any of those. Instead she set the boxes down carefully, lifted one of them and held it up in front of him.

'Take a look,' she said, lifting the box as close to his face as she could get it and suddenly unsnapping the cover, so that he got the full force of the rotting blood and day-old shit and urine and whatever other unmentionable and unimaginable things the women stuffed in there every day. The effect was total and immediate like a bomb hitting. BLOWIE. Blondie reeled backwards, automatically whipping out his snow-white handkerchief and clapping it to his nose, while his young companion suddenly retched and choked, as if zapped by an unexpected blast of poison gas.

'Good God,' he gasped in a half-strangulated croak, backing as far away as the confining walls of the lift would let him. 'What the hell is that?'

Sonia smiled sweetly at them, gathered up her boxes and got out of the lift as quickly as she could, but as she squeezed out of the opening door she couldn't resist a parting word, so she turned her head and smiled again.

'Bye-bye,' she said. 'I'll be back.'

Chapter 3

Byron got the message at reception when he was leaving the hospital next day. They had kept him in, 'for observation' they called it, although he hadn't noticed anyone observing him. But, as the doctor had said the night before, he had to expect a little confusion after falling out a window twenty floors up. The police had been and questioned him about what happened, but Byron knew better than to tell them the truth. He said he had been leaning out and somehow fell. There was a story in nearly every paper that morning about it, and Byron wished that he dared to tell them what really happened. But he knew very well that doing that would be the same as grassing, and he had a shrewd suspicion that after his miraculous escape, crossing Fergus again would be pushing his luck too far.

His instinct was to put all that behind him. He'd got out of the hospital as fast as he could because he had read that the driver on whose car he had landed was planning to pay him a visit, and he didn't fancy standing up to whatever hassle the man had in mind. A dislocated shoulder and a slightly sprained wrist hadn't been too high a price to pay he thought, but he had actually wrecked the guy's dodgy old Renault. When he'd landed on top of the car he'd blacked out for a minute, and then opened his eyes to find himself staring straight through the cracked windscreen at the horrified face of a middle-aged black man, who, oddly enough, instead of getting out and trying to help him, just sat there with his mouth wide open giving out scream after scream, unearthly howls as if he was being tortured. Byron woke up fully then, moved his limbs a little to see whether he could, slid off the car, and shouted, 'Shut up for God's sake.' The man had shut up and sat there watching him walk away as if he was a ghost. Unfortunately Byron only managed to take a few steps before he collapsed again, and when he woke up he was in an ambulance, speeding towards the hospital.

After that it wasn't too bad. At least he'd had a good night's sleep, and Byron reckoned that he had been even luckier than anyone knew because he couldn't think where he would have spent the night if he hadn't found himself in the nice clean hospital bed.

He had come back to the city simply to see Marie and the baby. But now something told him that the best thing he could do was to keep away from them, and that left him without a focus or direction. Putting his clothes on, he kept thinking about what to do next. Luckily Fergus must have thrown his bag through the window after him, because he found it in the locker next to him when he woke up. So he didn't have to worry about fetching that either. The only thing he regretted was that he hadn't got a chance to telephone the girl he'd met on the train. But, as it happened, the fall and the crash and the drugs they'd given him seemed to have quietened down his urges for the moment and when he thought about Katrina it was with no more than a feeling of mild nostalgia for what might have been.

So, when Byron read Sonia's message, it seemed like the finger of fate, pointing him in a new direction. What he ought to do, he thought, was go back down to London and see Sonia. He knew that Willie was there too and it made sense to go and check both of them out. After Hyacinth they were the nearest thing to a family he had. He couldn't count Marie any more, not after the bitch had nearly got him killed, and suddenly he felt deep inside him something like an irresistible longing to see Sonia.

He rang the number that she had left, but there was no reply, and all of a sudden he decided not to wait. It wasn't until an hour later and the train was thundering towards Crewe that he remembered the triplets, Louis, Mohammed and Ray, who he knew were also in Manchester and who he should have gone to right away. Louis, Mohammed and Ray were hard. They had once had a father, who'd named them after his boxing heroes and, in a way, it was a sort of prophecy, because the triplets had grown up harder than anyone else Byron knew, and they always had been, even as kids living together in the foster home. He had a feeling that even Fergus would have had to back off if confronted by those three. Perhaps he hadn't thought of that because somehow everything he'd been through had scrambled his brains, and he'd forgotten about them. But by now it was too late. He certainly couldn't bear the thought of going back, even if everything had been all right.

On the forecourt at Euston station Byron tried Sonia's number again. Still no answer. He sat down on the stairs at the side entrance to the station, opened his bag, fumbling with the sling round his left arm, and located the letter that Willie had written him. The address was somewhere in West London and Byron decided to go there straight away. At least Willie would fix him up with a bed for a while and he could relax and think a little. He had left Manchester on an impulse backed up by the shock of what had happened to him. But now he'd had time for it to sink in, he was beginning to realize that the only things he could call his own had been ripped away from him, and the way things were, it didn't seem as if there was any way of getting them back, not without killing Fergus, and he wasn't sure that he wanted to do that, even if he could.

Willie lived in a street off Harrow Road, not far from Westbourne Grove where Byron had got off the tube. He walked past a clutch of Indian shops, halal meat, yams and salt cod. On the corner a greengrocer's stall. Once he got off the main road, the street was quiet, with a row of squat three-storey houses which looked like cut-down versions of the big old houses you'd see in the part of Sheffield where he'd grown up. Willie opened the door when he knocked, and gave him a big grin. Byron felt his own face lighting up, in a reflection of Willie's delight.

'El Segundo,' Byron shouted, slapping his hand hard into Willie's outstretched palm, and then hugging him one-handed.

El Segundo was the nickname Louis, Mohammed and Ray had given Willie because he used to hang around behind Byron all the time like the gunslinger in a western they'd been to see once. The triplets themselves were always together every minute of the day and night, but as one of them always said when Willie protested, that was different.

Byron had expected Willie to be living in a room, or something like that. Willie wasn't officially out of the care of the social services and he was only sixteen, so when Willie led him through to the kitchen of the house, opened the fridge and poured him a beer Byron stared at him almost with his mouth open.

'What's this place?' he asked Willie. 'Is it a home or something?'

'No,' Willie beamed at him proudly. 'The house belongs to this woman I'm living with.'

Willie grinned proudly again at the amazement on Byron's face, and Byron smoothed his features into indifference. But over the next few minutes Willie told him the whole story.

A few months before, he had absconded and headed for London, because having grown up together with

Sonia and Byron he had been lonely and miserable once they left and stopped coming to see him. After all, they hadn't even telephoned. Shortly after he'd turned fifteen the foster-parents they had spent the longest time with died in an accident, so they put him back in a group house where he didn't get on with anyone, and as soon as he'd got up enough nerve he had split. The cops had picked him up in a squat in Paddington and, recognizing that he was under age, they were about to send him back when he'd been seen by this social worker who made the identical offer to him and two girls who were in the same position and had been picked up with him. They could stay in her house while they sorted themselves out. There was some kind of arrangement with the authorities, which was to do with the fact that he was close to sixteen years old, when he'd be released from care anyway. Back in Yorkshire the local authorities weren't red-hot to have him back, and once the social worker had offered to help with his transition from being in care to independence they'd been only too pleased to let him stay. It was their version of community care, his social worker had said. The two girls had been included in the deal, but it was only a matter of weeks before they disappeared one by one. One of them had turned sixteen and gone to live with a bloke up in Norwood, while the other one had simply got itchy feet, hopped on the train to Brighton one night and had never been seen again.

This left Willie all alone, sharing the house with the social worker, whose name was Vicky. She was about thirty-six, Willie thought, and not too long divorced, and he was, she told him, the only thing that kept her from going crazy rattling round in that big house all by herself. Willie got himself a job as a messenger riding round London on a mountain bike, a day-glo blue Muddy Fox, which Vicky bought him on condition he paid her back a bit every week. He felt like his own boss, and living there with Vicky made him feel like he'd found the best foster-home he'd ever been in. It wasn't long, either, before Vicky began treating him a bit like a mum, he thought, asking where he'd been when he came in late, and waking him up with a cup of tea in time to get to the dispatch office in the morning. But in a way, it was all too good to be true, and there was more to come.

Although life was good enough now for Willie, his patron Vicky couldn't conceal from him that she herself was still going through a bad time. She was definitely moody most days, and sometimes he would come into the room and find her sat by herself, crying. Or when he went past her bedroom on the way to the bathroom, sometimes he'd hear her voice behind the door, smashing things, and shouting and swearing, using words that he never heard her use in ordinary conversation. The funny thing was that, going about her normal routine, she always looked in control, a tall blonde, a bit bossy, with cold straight blue eyes, talked a bit posh, and Willie could see that blokes fancied her, though she didn't smile a lot or anything, so they'd have had to be real cool themselves to try anything on. But she didn't seem to have much of a life outside her work. Her parents were dead and she didn't have any brothers and sisters, just an ex-husband who had become a successful businessman and gone off with another woman. She had a couple of pals, women she'd known since her university days, she said. They only came to see her occasionally, and soon after Willie moved in one of them had married and immediately given birth to a baby, which seemed to anger Vicky considerably, and after that she never came round any more.

Willie didn't know what to do about Vicky's moods, and in any case he wasn't too bothered; being a kid, it wasn't his problem. But as he began to feel his own independence and the sense that he too was an adult, he began to get more concerned about Vicky and to wonder more often just what was wrong with her, and one night sitting at the kitchen table after he had come in and found her up, staring at the TV with the sound turned off, he asked straight out why she was so miserable.

'It's a year since my divorce,' Vicky said. 'You'll understand more about it when you're older. We started to have a child but it died, and soon affter that we broke up. I don't know why, but it's hard to get over it. You'll understand when you're older.'

But Willie knew all about that sort of thing anyway, he told her. He had lived in more than one foster-home where the mother had lost children or not been able to have them or it had ended in the couple breaking up. In a way Willie thought all of that was so normal that it surprised him a little Vicky was taking it so hard. But when he told her all this, trying to comfort her, Vicky only started crying again.

'Oh God,' Vicky said, 'I'm such a pathetic old bag feeling sorry for myself, when other people are so badly off.'

Any other time Willie would have laughed out loud at this, because he could have told her that anyone who sat about worrying about how badly off other people were was an idiot. One thing he'd learnt was look after number one. But he had determined to be a comfort to her. At the back of his mind was the thought that he wanted to stay here as long as he could, and if Vicky could come to regard him as part of her family he'd be safe. So he told her that she wasn't pathetic, and how grateful he was for everything she was doing for him, and after that she cheered up a little, and they had a long talk till the early hours of the morning.

After that night Willie and Vicky had become closer and more interested in each other, like a bit of a team, Willie thought, the way he'd been with Byron and Sonia.

The differences between them didn't seem to matter, especially sitting in the kitchen late at night, all shut away and private from the rest of the world, and somehow, now he could talk to her about ordinary things like the funny people he ran into during the day, Vicky didn't seem so old and aloof as she had at the beginning. They got so friendly that one night, on Vicky's birthday, Willie decided to cook her dinner. Cooking wasn't his strong point but he got the dishes from Marks and Spencer's food counter, and when they came out of the oven and he stuck them on the plate they looked fantastic. Vicky was touched that Willie had remembered, and that being the sort of teenager he was had gone to the trouble of doing something for her. No one had been nice to her in that way for quite a long time, she thought.

In any case she had found Willie sweet and attractive right from the beginning, in the way teenage boys could be, but seldom were. He had a thin, sensitive face, with a hint of sadness and confusion about the eyes, the sort of look that used to make girls swoon over James Dean, and probably still did, and there was something about him which made you want to mother him as soon as you saw him. So she sat and made out to enjoy it all because Willie must have spent well over ten pounds on the dinner, and even though she didn't much like salmon she ate it enthusiastically and praised him repeatedly. Under the influence of all the good cheer she opened the bottle of champagne they'd given her at the office and she and Willie drank it all, then went on to a bottle of red wine she'd brought back from France the year before.

By round about one in the morning they were both rolling drunk. Afterwards Vicky blamed the fact that she was pissed as a newt, but since she was a pretty honest person she also guessed that this was a bit of an excuse. The truth was that she'd been noticing for a while that Willie was a big boy for his age. He was nearly six foot and it was clear he was going to be an impressive figure of a man and good-looking with it too. With all that he was sweet-natured and touchingly grateful, and dependent on her for almost everything. It was a bit, she guessed, like having a teenage son without the terrible trouble that teenage sons seemed to give most mothers. On the other hand it wasn't.

As they drank the wine round the rubble of her birthday dinner Vicky did notice that Willie was eyeing her breasts in a way which reminded her that she hadn't been in bed with a man for a couple of years. Not that she was unattractive. Let's get that straight, she said to herself. In fact she'd had plenty of offers, especially when her colleagues and acquaintances knew she was splitting up with her husband. For some reason she hadn't been able, except for one occasion which she preferred to forget, to indulge herself by accepting any of them, but suddenly, sitting there with Willie, she'd started to feel something remarkably like an urgent desire to feel his arms round her and his youthful muscles pressing up against her and inside her. So that night when they'd finally got up, both of them staggering a little, Vicky couldn't resist offering him a little kiss for, as she put it, being such a good boy. She had meant simply to give him an affectionate embrace and a kiss to see what it felt like. But somehow the kiss lasted longer than she had intended and before long she and Willie were locked together, his massive young dick grinding in the valley of her thighs, her tongue swirling about in his mouth, and his eager hands squeezing her breasts so hard that it would have been painful if she had been capable of feeling pain at that moment. Not long after, Willie was in her bed, lying on top of her and pumping vigorously between her outstretched legs. As Willie came inside her, groaning loudly, Vicky reflected that it had been a long time since she'd had it so good.

Next day she woke up with a feeling of sheer horror. She had violated a rigid taboo, and if anyone found out she would probably be in a heap of trouble at work. She could imagine the reactions of the colleagues she'd turned down if they found out that she had gone to bed with a sixteen-year-old absconder and laboured enthusiastically over his body until she'd fallen asleep exhausted. It didn't bear thinking about.

That morning she sat Willie down in the kitchen, and swore him to silence, and told him it must never happen again or he would have to leave. Willie agreed, and apologized, although she told him there was no need to because it was her fault. Then he got on his bike and set off for the dispatch office in a daze. This wasn't a reaction to his first sexual experience, because it hadn't actually been Willie's first experience. He'd done it before with a fourteen-year-old runaway who'd been in the hostel he was living in. She had charged him two pounds the first time but later on she let him for only a quid, when he got smart enough to say he couldn't afford it. But this was different.

Vicky was a grown woman and beautiful, with big ripe tits and a body which seemed to welcome him softly, like sinking into bed after a long hard day. Of course Willie had been aware before that Vicky turned him on, but he'd known that it was impossible that she would ever let a kid like himself touch her, so he'd contented himself with jerking off quietly at night while he thought about what her naked body would be like. The fact that she'd let him do what he had done during the dark hours till the birds started singing outside seemed like a miraculous gift from God, and all through the day Willie felt like laughing and crying alternately. He fully intended to do what Vicky had said, that was, to forget about it and keep his hands to himself in future, but by the time he got home he had the most incredible erection bulging the front of the lycra bike shorts he wore all day.

Even then Willie tried. Vicky wasn't home yet so he had a wank then showered in cold water and, somewhat calmer, wanked himself off again. The trouble was that Vicky didn't come back all evening. She rang up to say that she was going to a meeeting, and then out for a drink with some friends and that he ought to have his dinner and go to bed without waiting up for her. Willie guessed that she was trying to avoid him that evening, in case of anything happening, and he thought that this must be the sensible and grown-up thing to do. So he went to bed early, wanked himself off some more and went to sleep. He meant to greet her in the morning, and pretend as if nothing had happened. But it didn't work out like that, because Willie woke up around about two in the morning, dying for a pee. He got up and went to the bathroom. Behind Vicky's bedroom door the light was off, but he could tell she was in there because the door was now firmly closed. Coming back from the bathroom, with only a T-shirt on, the way he usually slept, Willie thought of Vicky lying in bed and his dick made a sudden bound, stretching out in front of him like a rigid horizontal bar. He went past to his own room, then turned back. He would just check on Vicky, he thought, and see whether she was all right. So he tapped softly on her door, and went in. Vicky hadn't answered when he knocked but when he went into the darkness of the room and whispered, 'Vicky it's me. Are you sleeping?' he heard her stir. 'No,' she said shortly. Willie felt his way to the bed.

'You're back then,' he said. 'You all right?' 'Yes,' Vicky whispered in reply. 'Go back to your room.' The sound of her voice, nomally so confident and authoritative, was weak and quavering, and Willie kept moving forward, meaning to sit on the edge of the bed and reassure her that she needn't be afraid that he would say anything or take advantage of her kindness, but instead he found himself lying full length on top of Vicky, and the miracle happened again. Vicky's legs parted slowly, she put her arms round him and he was inside her.

After that night Vicky gave up trying to stop it happening. Neither of them thought very much any more about what would happen next, or what would happen if Vicky's friends and bosses knew what she was doing with Willie. Luckily she didn't lead a busy social life anyway, so the opportunities for anyone finding out the true state of affairs were strictly limited. Willie didn't think about her as a mum any more, and Vicky didn't think about him as a son, but on the other hand they didn't know quite how to think about each other.

This was the story Willie poured out into Byron's unbelieving ears, as they sat supping lager from the fridge that afternoon.

Chapter 4

Byron rang Sonia's number a couple of hours later, and this time she answered the phone.

'Byron,' she screamed. She couldn't believe that it was actually his voice. 'Where are you? Have you got a phone there?'

'I'm in London,' he said.

'You can't be,' Sonia screamed at him. 'I thought you'd be in hospital. Are you all right? Did you break anything?'

'No,' Byron said sort of cool. 'I bounced, didn't I.'

Sonia couldn't stop laughing and she insisted that Byron came round to her house right away. In any case, she said, she was being evicted the next day and she didn't know where she would be so it was best that they made contact that night.

This just about suited Willie, because, although he had told Byron he could stay in the house as long as he liked, he wasn't sure that it would be all right with Vicky, and he wanted Byron away out of the house when she came back so that he could tell her about him and make sure that she didn't mind having him around for a few days.

Byron arrived round at Sonia's about half-past six. Sonia opened the door, threw her arms round him, jumped up and wrapped her legs round his waist the way she used to when she was a kid, and Byron carried her back into the flat that way draped all round him and kissing him frantically round his neck. He dumped her in the hallway as soon as he got the door closed.

'Bloody hell,' Byron said, grinning at her. 'You've put on some weight. Grown up into a big girl.'

She was such a big girl, in fact, although he didn't tell her this, that when she'd jumped up on him his body had reacted immediately in a most unbrotherly way, because at that moment Sonia had felt more like a big armful of squirming woman than the little sister he remembered.

She'd been spooning heaps of yukky carrot-coloured stuff into the baby's mouth, which Juliet didn't seem to mind, even though she seemed to have most of the stuff smeared round her mouth and on her little bib.

'I'm taking her round to Missis Holland's in a minute,' Sonia told him. 'She's going to have her tonight because I've got to sort things out and get my stuff away early in the morning. They served me notice a week ago but I only managed to get another place today.'

What she didn't tell him was that the place she'd got as a temporary refuge was a room in Charlie's house, and she hoped she'd only have to stop there a couple of days before she located another squat or found a place that was cheap enough to rent. An hour later they were sitting in a nearby pub. Apart from being thrilled at seeing Byron once again, Sonia also felt as if she hadn't been able to talk to anyone for years, not in the way she could talk to Byron, and she began giving him the story of more or less everything that had happened to her since he'd left the home. In Byron's case this was nearly four years, so there was a lot of ground to cover, but Sonia rattled on and on, telling him about how she'd shared a flat in Nottingham with three other girls who'd been released from care at the same time, and how after a couple of years she got fed up of working in supermarkets, and she'd hit the road to London. But the first thing that happened was she fell in love, or she thought she was in love, with a man who picked her up on the train where he was coming back with his mates from a football match in Leeds. He was a professional footballer, at least he was in the reserves at Palace, and it looked as if he had a bright future. He reckoned, anyway, that he was better than John Barnes, and more sensible than Ian Wright, and better looking than Paul Ince. But half-way through her pregnancy he had done his knee in, and even before the baby was born, it was all over. He'd gone back to his wife, who he'd left when he thought he was going to be successful, and although at first he'd seen Sonia regularly and dropped her a few quid for the baby, he'd stopped coming in the end. Then when she went round to his address she found that the couple had gone, without leaving a forwarding address. For a few days she had gone round in a state of misery and rage, but eventually she'd had to get herself together and start thinking about how to fend for herself and the baby.

Byron listened to all this with a sense of amazement and growing dislocation. He was only twenty himself, and he knew how violent and dramatic the changes were that went on in your life after sixteen, and before you got to more advanced ages like twenty-one. But he was accustomed to thinking of Sonia as a little girl, and all of this was like an overload of weird life-coloured images zapping straight into his brain. But even stranger were Sonia's stories about her job.

'What it is,' Sonia said, 'it's not healthy. You know what I mean? People always reckon that the worse thing is like going in the toilet and picking up them boxes. And that's bad enough. By the end of the day you're covered in sweat, and the boxes keep slipping out of your hands and it's like murder, man. But going back to the depot what happens, it's like this. You have to empty all the boxes in a big pile in the middle of the floor like a little mountain of used tampons, all stiff and fat and stinking. And there's these women, man, I mean they wear gloves but that's not the point. They have to pick them up and put them in these black plastic bags and then they take them down to the incinerator. You just imagine being stood there all day crouched over the tampons shovelling them back and forth and carrying these heavy bags back and forth and all. I mean the smell's the worst. You don't wanna smell that, mate. But it's not all that bad in winter. That's the thing, at least it's cold. It's worst in summer because there's none of your air-conditioning, and you can imagine how bad the stink gets. Sometimes one of the women faints and just falls on her face into the tampons. I mean people have got no idea.'

Byron nodded, spellbound over his pint of draught. It was true he'd had no idea, although it was something you could have worked out if you thought about it, and so far he'd thought that slopping out, walking to the toilet in the morning with a bucket full of shit and piss in your hand, was the most degrading thing he could think of. But he reckoned that this had it beat by a long way.

'Mind you,' Sonia continued, 'it's quite interesting really. You wouldn't believe,' she said, 'what happens in some of these places. I usually pick up at this shopping mall in Epsom. It's dead posh when you drive through, and there's all these women in hats and that, with dogs on leashes, driving about in Land-Rovers and all that. But number one the lavvies are just as disgusting or more as anywhere else, and the other thing is they stick bottles in the containers. Gin, vodka, wine, all sorts. I mean I'm weighed down with bottles when I come out of there. What I reckon is, they're all boozing at home, and instead of putting the bottles out for the dustmen to find, or their husbands or whatever, they go down the old shopping mall, and Bob's your uncle, never mind the girl who's got to pick them up. Spose they think it's just like having a shit, pull the chain and it's gone.'

Byron looked at Sonia, his jaw dropping with amazement. For a start he'd hardly got a word in edgewise so far. But the other thing was that he still couldn't get over how grown-up she was. It was only later on that it occurred to him, and months later Sonia confirmed it, that she was nervous, both about meeting him again after such a long time, and about the fact that he'd been in prison. She just didn't know whether she ought to ask about it or not, and talking about herself the way she had was one way of avoiding such difficulties. Also, she did like to talk, and what is more, as she told him, she had a lot more to say.

'How come you're doing this job then?' Byron asked.

It was all because, Sonia told him, her expression growing angry and bitter, she'd been chucked out of this really good job that she had before. What it was had been a big betting shop. She'd got the job when Juliet was a couple of months old and she'd found this lady near the squat she'd got into, who was really good and had some children of her own, so she didn't mind looking after little Jools as long as she got paid regular. Sonia had enjoyed the job. It was different to supermarkets, not so boring, and because the shop was in the West End of London it was miles better than your usual run of betting shops, and some of the people who came in were really quite high class, such as a couple of actors who you saw on telly, like him who acted the detective on Saturday nights, then there was another man who used to be a well-known footballer, and some people who thought nothing of dropping up to five hundred quid a day. Chinese mostly. Of course you got the usual maniacs and alcoholics, but usually they were nice and whenever any of the big players won a few he'd most likely slip her a fiver or sometimes as much as a tenner for herself.

The complication was the manager, George. George Crooks was his name, funnily enough. He was an older bloke, probably over forty, she reckoned, although she wasn't sure, and from the time she went there he started chatting her up. There were usually two or three other women in the shop, but they were all middle-aged, married or living with blokes, and, as it turned out later, George was probably only on to her because she was the only one who was available, young and pretty. Anyway, she hadn't paid much attention to his fooling around at first, because he was married and she didn't really fancy him that much to be honest. But after a few weeks, in which he paid her continual attention, taking her out for a drink when they worked late, and buying her little presents, giving her a lift home and asking after Juliet in a serious, friendly way, she began to loosen up towards him, and their relationship progressed from an amicable peck when he dropped her off to long French kissing during which his hands would wander over her breasts squeezing gently. After a week or so of this she was hot anyway, and one night when she stayed overtime with him to cover the late racing, he had locked the door after the last punter had gone home, and while she was making up her face in front of the little mirror in the office at the back where they made tea and went to sit down for a break, he had come up behind her, put his hands on her breasts, squeezed and stroked them in that special way he had, then put his hands under the hem of her skirt and between her legs, and bent her over and pushed gently but irresistibly right into her. That first time they had done it exactly like that, Sonia leaning forward with her elbows against the wall, her legs wide apart, while George screwed her vigorously from behind.

After that she got quite a lot of overtime, and she and George did it everywhere they could, in the office after they'd closed up, before they opened and on the way home in the car. She liked George and although he could never spare much more time than it took to give her one, he was nice and for a while she felt that she was passionately and romantically in love with him. But things had changed.

About a couple of weeks before she lost her job, she noticed that George was suddenly finding it more and more difficult to get the time for being alone with her, and for doing what they had done so often before. For some reason it never occurred to her that he might have had enough or that he'd gone off her. So she could not have been more shocked and hurt when she came in early one day dressed in a calf-length skirt with a split up the side, and no panties underneath, to give him a pleasant surprise, and heard his voice grunting in the unmistakable throes of sexual frenzy. She opened the door of the office quietly and saw that George, his trousers and the red boxer shorts she'd given him down around his ankles, was sitting back in the armchair, while Terry, the new girl he'd just taken on, a brassy little bottle-blonde tart just left school, was kneeling at his feet fellating him furiously.

Sonia just screamed. Unfortunately for George neither he nor Terry had heard or seen Sonia's approach and, convulsed with the shock of the sudden noise, Terry's jaw had clamped shut on his dick giving him a painful and temporarily incapacitating bite. For the rest of the day George limped around giving her evil looks. Terry was sent off early, giving Sonia a sly and haughty leer as she teetered off on her stilettos. Then next day the area manager came to see her, told her that her work was unsatisfactory, gave her a week's pay in lieu of notice, and she was back on the street without a job that afternoon.

She had heard later than Terry had spent a couple of weeks as holiday relief for the area manager and she hoped she was having to spend most of her time on her knees in front of the smelly old git, but that didn't help her situation. She had to have a job right away, and when the Job Centre gave her the card for the women-only waste disposal depot she had jumped at it.

'I didn't know, did I?' Sonia said.

Byron agreed with her, the way he'd been doing all night. By then it was nearly eleven, and he told her he had to be getting back to Willie's place. Sonia tried to persuade him to come back with her and help pack her stuff for the morning, but Byron reckoned that he had to get back early enough to meet Willie's landlady and get himself settled in, so they arranged to meet the next day and pick up where they'd left off. She hadn't found out anything about what was happening with him, Sonia said, because he'd let her shoot her mouth off so much, but Byron told her that there was plenty of time to talk about all that, and they parted with a big hug, and Byron watched Sonia swaying off down the road, feeling that he'd underestimated life on the outside, because when he came to think about it the last couple of days since he'd been released had been the strangest period of his life so far. That was saying something, and the day wasn't over yet.

Chapter 5

The first thing Byron didn't like about Vicky was that she asked him a lot of questions. The second thing was that she frightened him. Up to the very last moment he knew Vicky, there was something about her which made him feel that at any moment she might tell him off, in a way that would make him feel small, leaving him angry and ashamed. The point was that Vicky was a social worker and she understood exactly what kind of person Byron was because she had seen hundreds like him, every detail complete, even down to his charm, his hard luck story, and the bulge in his jeans. If she knew one thing about his type it was that Byron was on a fast road to nowhere, and while she loved and trusted Willie from the beginning, because she thought he was young enough to be different and she could save him from that kind of future, with Byron she felt the opposite, and from the way he eyed her under his respectful manner, she knew that Willie had told him everything and that he was watching her carefully, working out how and where she was vulnerable, and calculating steadfastly how and for how much he could take her.

But she had known all this, she told herself, and already been resigned to it from the moment Willie opened his mouth to tell her that Byron had turned up and could he stay for a couple of days till he got himself sorted out. She'd said yes of course, because it would have been too much of a problem to explain to Willie just what she knew and suspected about his best friend and childhood hero, even before she met him. The trouble was that she'd put off doing something about sorting out the situation with Willie, because, unless she thought about how it would look to other people, she was happier than she'd been for a long time and she felt that she really owed it to herself. She thought sometimes that she really ought to discuss it with someone and the only person she could imagine talking to about this was her best friend Jill, who was headmistress of a primary school in Highgate, but the idea of talking to Jill turned her off as soon as it came into her head because she knew that Jill would say she was stark raving mad, and that it was all something to do with the trauma of divorce. Vicky didn't want to hear Jill say that, because she could work it out just as easily for herself and knowing it didn't help.

The trouble was, as Byron told Willie next day when Vicky had gone to work, and Willie had popped back between messages to see whether he was all right, Vicky reminded him of a lot of the people who'd been in charge of their lives till that point. It was true that she was dead tasty, and how old she was didn't matter much, she had everything a man could want, and he guessed that Willie knew that better than anyone, but she was like definitely one of those people who had grown up telling other people what to do, and she had the bossiness to prove it.

For instance, as soon as Byron had come in the house, she started asking him things like what he'd been done for, and when he had to see his probation officer, and both of these were things that Byron wanted not to have to think about. But when she pressed him, he had looked her straight in the eye to check out her reaction to what she was hearing, and told her clearly and in detail how he had robbed a post office, with two idiots up in Chorlton. The couple who ran it were pretty old, so they hadn't been expecting any trouble, and Steve, who fancied himself as some kind of gang leader, had insisted that they should carry replica guns. Just show it to them he reckoned, and they'll shit themselves. No problem. But instead of shivering with terror and handing over the contents of the safe, the old lady had looked at Steve's gun and sussed right away that it wasn't real. She'd hit some kind of alarm and then whacked Steve across the face with her handbag. Afterwards it was in all the papers about this brave old lady fighting off three hulking young robbers, but the fact was that she had scared them half out of their lives, coming at them like an insane old bat screaming, shouting, clawing and hitting out in every direction with her lethal leather cosh. The whole thing had been a joke, but instead of laughing the judge had given Steve and Kevin a couple of years each. Byron, being the black one, had got another year on top of that. He should have known better, Byron told himself every day he was inside, but by then it was much too late.

Vicky listened to all this without expression. Willie laughed when he told them about the old lady, and watched him with big eyes of sympathy when he talked about being banged up, while Byron watched them both. But then Vicky had started on at him, and said that she wasn't responsible for what he did but that she didn't want Willie involved in anything dodgy, and that if she saw the first sign that he was doing anything he shouldn't, he would be out and if Willie didn't like it he would be out too. In any case she was only giving him a week or so till he got on his feet.

Byron took all this with a smile and nodded as if he agreed she was being dead reasonable, but inside he was not much pleased. Vicky was coming on exactly like all the authorities he'd ever encountered and he wondered if he should tell her how hypocritical she sounded, shagging the life out of little Willie and making out like she was something special. But while Byron was uncomfortable with Vicky, and he couldn't predict what trouble she might cause him if he did anything out of order, he still liked being in the house with Willie. There were three bedrooms and an empty basement, room for all the kids in the house where he'd grown up, so he reckoned it would be a pretty good place to stay while he thought what to do, and he didn't want to risk getting kicked out by upsetting Vicky for nothing, so he determined to act polite, keep out of her way, and avoid saying anything that might get up her nose.

The next day he just relaxed and took it easy. That afternoon after Willie came home they sat around, talking. He told Willie about what it had felt like to be locked up, and how he had been overpowered by the dread Fergus. Then they got to reminiscing about the days when Willie was El Segundo and they'd been living with the triplets and Sonia. Later on they went out and bought fish and chips the way they used to, coming back in and smothering the chips in tomato ketchup. By this time Vicky had got home from work, but she didn't trouble them, having her dinner by herself, some kind of salad, all raw vegetables, sitting in the room where she had her books, which she and Willie called her study, writing some kind of social worker stuff, and all she said before she went to bed was to remind Willie to lock up and turn the lights off. Byron showed Willie the fist after she'd gone out of the door, sticking his tongue out and wagging it round, but Willie hadn't joined in. As a matter of act he looked a bit moody when Byron did that, so Byron left off and didn't say any more about Vicky because he wasn't sure that Willie wouldn't side with her if push came to shove. But apart from that Willie was the same good kid he always was, and altogether it was a good day, so that by the time Byron went to bed he was feeling that he'd run into the first piece of real good luck that he'd had for a number of years.

Meanwhile, Sonia was going through what she described to Byron and Willie later on as a living hell.

This was an exaggeration, typical of Sonia, as they found out later. But even so, when she told them the story it sounded pretty strong.

Sonia had borrowed a van from the depot early, promising Charlie and Vange that she would be back in less than an hour, and she was. Then she had dropped her stuff off in a corner of the big warehouse, while she went out on the day's pick-ups. Everything seemed to be going smoothly, and by that evening she was safely installed in the attic at Charlie's house, giving Juliet her dinner and putting her to bed. Later on she went down to watch the telly and make a few phone calls to try to locate somewhere to stay, although Charlie assured her that there'd be no problem stopping for a bit until she got on her feet. But by then she'd realized that the real problem was being there and coping with Charlie and Charlie's little ways. For a start, Charlie, and Charlie's house, weren't exactly too hygienic, and the kitchen sink, the kitchen table and every other available surface was piled high or littered with dirty dishes, old takeaway cartons, cat litter and cat dishes caked and crusted with unidentifiable old meat. The fridge too was full of tins of cat food, and Sonia had to clear a space to make room for Juliet's baby food. In the corner near the fridge there was a tray of cat litter from which the smell of cat piss pervaded the lower floors of the house.

'They're only cats,' Charlie said laughing when Sonia mentioned it. 'It's not as if it was human urine, is it?'

To be fair, Charlie had probably become desensitized to the smell by now, but to someone with a normal nose it was almost overpowering, and Sonia could hardly bear to go near the kitchen, much less cook anything in it. On top of all that, Charlie had got more and more affectionate as the night wore on. Sonia had shoved three of the cats – as far as she could make out there were about seven – off the sofa to make room for herself while she watched *EastEnders*, and half-way through Charlie had come up and sat next to her, her bulk filling the available space and pressing uneasily against Sonia. This was what Sonia had been afraid of, and after she'd moved over a couple of inches, until the arm of the sofa stopped her going any further and she was squashed half breathless in the tiny space left by Charlie's sweating bulk, she got up and announced that she was going upstairs to check on Juliet. Once upstairs she closed the door and lay on the bed. She couldn't stay, she knew that now. Being sat up in the dingy attic room all night, hiding from Charlie, would drive her raving mad, she thought. But worse was to come.

In about an hour, when, she guessed, Charlie had realized she wasn't coming back down, she heard the street door slam and from the small attic window saw Charlie marching off down the road. Sonia breathed a sigh of relief, because she desperately wanted to go to the loo and one of the first things she'd discovered about the house was that not only was there no lock on the door of the bathroom, but someone had kicked or punched the panels of the door in, so that standing at the bottom of the stairs you could see whoever was on the loo at any time. This had made it impossible for Sonia to go all the while that Charlie was in the house. It wasn't that she was bothered about having Charlie see her having a pee or doing a dump, when she thought about it. It was just that she couldn't go.

After a while she'd got ready for bed and gone to sleep. One thing about the hard physical work she did was that when her head hit the pillow she was out like a light and usually she slept like a log, till Juliet woke her round about half five or six. But tonight was different. She woke when the street door slammed a couple of times, and there was a confused battle of noise from downstairs. The doors kept slamming, and women's voices shouted and bellowed snatches of song. She waited for it to end but it went on and on, rising to a peak from time to time. She wasn't particularly sensitive to noise herself but she knew that sooner or later Juliet would wake up and then it would be hell getting her back to sleep. She lay back, every muscle tensed, willing her daughter to stay asleep, but in a short time it happened. Juliet opened her eyes, looked around wonderingly, then sat up and began to cry. Sonia went over and cuddled her for a bit. She usually resisted taking her into her bed, because she thought once she started she wouldn't be able to stop, but eventually she took Juliet in her arms and lay back holding her till she drifted off again. In the meantime the noise had moderated a little, but suddenly Sonia felt in desperate need of a pee. She knew what the problem was. She hadn't been at her usual time just before she went to bed and now her bladder was bursting and she had to go. Cautiously she went down the flight of stairs to the bathroom. Down below she could hear Charlie and her friends. She wasn't sure what they were doing but from the erratic sounds which were emerging from the sitting-room she could make a good guess. Carefully she pinned a big towel over the holes in the door, then sat down for a piddle. So far so good, but this was when Sonia made her mistake. Somehow, as she sat on the loo, the idea flashed into her mind that she would like to have a peek at whatever it was they were doing down there. She tried to put the idea out of her mind, but it kept coming back and soon she was giggling to herself at the thought of seeing big Charlie with her mates on the job, she'd look so silly. That was it. She couldn't resist, and when she'd finished on the loo, instead of going back upstairs, she tiptoed warily downstairs, intending to peek through the half-open door and clear off again before they saw her. The plan might have worked, if Sonia had merely taken a quick look and left. As it was she got as far as looking, but then was transfixed by the sight of Charlie wielding a monstrously thick and long black vibrator which she was inserting with what seemed like an unnecessarily ferocious energy between the outspread thighs of a woman who was lying back on the sofa with her legs raised. Nearby another woman was sitting up on the other arm of the sofa dressed only in a black T-shirt, her legs outspread, her face a fixed and grinning mask of insane lust, her hand flying about rapidly in her steaming crotch. Sonia turned to go before they could see her but she was too late.

'Oi,' shouted the woman on the arm of the sofa, 'what you looking at then?'

'Leave her alone, Rocky,' Charlie grunted, but Rocky was already off the sofa, and running towards Sonia. For a moment Sonia nearly turned and ran at the sight of Rocky rushing towards her, her huge tits flopping up and down, her big spotty face plastered with tendrils of greasy black hair, and still grinning with something of the mad glare Sonia had seen just a moment before. At that point Sonia was really a bit terrified, but she thrust away the idea of running the moment it crossed her mind. If she ran Rocky might chase her, and she didn't fancy bursting into the bedroom where Juliet was lying asleep with this big animal after her. So instead of retreating she stood still, and held her hands up in a traffic stopping gesture.

'All right,' Sonia said, as calmly as she could. 'I'm not up for this lot. OK?'

In the past, whenever she'd encountered situations like this, she had found that it was enough to say something of the kind, but even while the words were coming out she realized that she'd have trouble with Rocky, because the woman was reeling drunk, Sonia could smell it half-way across the room, and Rocky was in no mood to be reasoned with.

'Go on,' Rocky said, leering. 'Not a virgin, are you?'

At the same time she closed on Sonia, grabbing her by her buttocks and pulling her up against her damp and streaming body. Unfortunately Sonia had come down wearing only the man's shirt she'd got from Juliet's dad, and when Rocky grabbed her she remembered that she was completely naked and vulnerable below the waist. But she soon had more to worry about. Crushed between the wall and Rocky's enfolding flesh Sonia felt she was being smothered. Even worse, she was getting the full blast of Rocky's reeking breath from her open mouth as it came towards her, the seeking tongue licking and rasping across her neck, leaving a trail of slimy saliva on her skin.

'Leave off,' Sonia shouted angrily, pushing with all her strength against Rocky's bulk. Sonia was a strong girl but it was no use. Rocky was so big, and aroused as she was Sonia was reduced to squirming feebly while the questing hands probed and rubbed roughly around her crotch. She tried to kick out, but that was no use either, and Sonia was just getting desperate at the thought of what Rocky might do to her next, when Charlie came to the rescue, coming up behind her friend and slapping her round the side of the head without ceremony. Rocky let go and looked at Charlie towering behind her with an air of hurt innocence.

'What'd you do that for?' she asked in an aggrieved tone.

'Piss off upstairs, Sonia,' Charlie said roughly. Then she put her arm round the shoulders of her friend, who by now had begun to cry, led her back into the sitting-room, and closed the door behind them. Sonia climbed the stairs slowly, half-way up hearing Juliet begin to scream. Tomorrow morning, she told herself, no messing about. I'm gone.

Chapter 6

Next morning Charlie was not in a good temper. As Sonia got Juliet ready to go over to Mrs Holland's, she muttered that the scene last night had well got on her nerves. If Sonia was going to stop there, Charlie told her, she'd damn well better not creep about the place spying. Either that or she'd better be prepared to join in with whatever was going on. The last thing Charlie wanted to do anyway, she said, was to risk her friendships on Sonia's account. Sonia let her finish grumbling, then told her that she needn't worry, she was going to move in with another friend for a while. This was a barefaced lie, but Sonia wasn't going to take all that moody first thing in the morning. In any case, she wanted to clear off and she reckoned she would do it by hook or by crook. Charlie took it with a sceptical look, but she obviously didn't want to stop Sonia. In fact she went so far as to offer the loan of a van later on so that Sonia could move her stuff, which made it all official.

Sonia felt a kind of relief at having made the decision to free herself from a situation which she imagined could only end badly. She didn't know what she would do next, but she guessed she would sort it all out during the day. She had an idea that she might now be eligible for council accommodation, and if the worst came to the worst, she could buy her way into sharing a house with a couple of the other women at the depot who'd been looking for somewhere to stay last time she'd heard. With this thought in mind she started the day figuring that she wasn't in bad shape, and even if she had to stay in bed and breakfast for a while, things would be sorted in a couple of days. But within a couple of hours she had lost her job, and all her calculations were up the creek. It wasn't anything to do with what had happened the night before. Charlie wasn't like that. Say what you like about the woman, Sonia had to admit, she might be an old bag, but she didn't bear a grudge, and in a way, she had been as kind as she knew how. So Sonia couldn't complain, because to some extent, and from Charlie's point of view, her sacking was completely justifiable.

How it happened was an accident, but really, the fact that it happened at all was down to the rain. For instance, if it hadn't been raining Sonia wouldn't have been in such a hurry to dump the pile of boxes containing the used tampons into the back of the van; and if she hadn't been in such a hurry she would have checked the doors, which on that particular van didn't close properly unless you jiggled them. Then, if it hadn't been raining, the traffic wouldn't have been so heavy that she had to put on a sudden spurt so as to pull out, after waiting for several long minutes for someone to pause and let her go. Also, if it hadn't been raining, the old lady wouldn't have slipped off the pavement into the traffic so that Sonia had to brake suddenly, springing open the back doors of the van; and if it hadn't been raining the van wouldn't have skidded so that she had to tromp on the brakes again, throwing the loosely stacked boxes out through the back into the road where they burst open, spattering their contents into the puddles of water.

From the vantage point of the van's side mirror the mess on the road looked like the results of some weird disaster. As Sonia watched, a woman, scurrying along under her umbrella, stumbled over one of the boxes, spilling tampons all over the pavement, and recoiled in shock as she realized what she was looking at. Someone screamed, and someone else shouted angrily. That did it.

Sonia had entertained a vague idea about going back to clear up, but at that point she winced, put it out of her head, and drove rapidly away.

The van had no markings, so she guessed she had probably got away with it, but that afternoon, when she drove in to the depot and saw Charlie clambering down the stairs like an avenging angel, her face set in a mask of rage, she knew that she hadn't.

'You're bloody sacked,' Charlie screamed, as Sonia got out of the van.

The police had been round, it turned out, and Vange herself had been forced to go down and sort it all out, the firm would be prosecuted, and it would cost them money, never mind the goodwill. Even Charlie herself could have been out on her ear over Sonia's little accident.

By the time Sonia picked up Jools that afternoon, she was desperate, but when she phoned Byron, from a phone booth near Clapham Common, and told him everything that had happened that day, he didn't hesitate.

'Come over here right now,' he said.

This was how Sonia arrived that evening at Vicky's house, with all her belongings stacked into a minicab and carrying Juliet in her arms.

Thinking about it later on, what struck Vicky was the fact that she felt very little surprise when she came home to see a litter of boxes in the hallway, and in the kitchen a mixed-race girl spooning pastel-coloured gunk into a screaming baby's mouth. She felt irritation, frustration, a spike of rage, a weird tinge of tenderness, and a hint of apprehension about Sonia's unexpected appearance, but as she stood in the doorway watching Willie and Byron trying to distract the child so that Sonia could get enough of the stuff into her mouth, she felt practically no surprise at all.

She'd been expecting something of the sort to happen

from the moment that Byron had appeared, and her first reaction was to wonder how she was going to tackle this new thing. Willie had leapt up, full of anxiety about what she would say, and before she could speak, he started introducing her to Sonia, and explaining her presence, stumbling over his words, his eyes skittering away from hers and then flashing back in urgent appeal. Vicky kept her expression carefully blank, so that Willie couldn't guess that while he talked as fast as he could, torn between his loyalty to his friends and the need to placate her, she had never liked him so much as at that moment.

In the end she said that Sonia could stay for a few days while she sorted herself out. Byron had already proposed, with an air of generosity, that if Vicky let her stay, she could occupy his room. Vicky noted his use of the possessive with an ironic lift of the eyebrow, but she didn't comment, and in a couple of hours Sonia was settled in, as comfortably as if she'd been there for ages. The funny thing was, Vicky also noted, how easily the three friends adapted to the new situation. She had intended getting Sonia into her study and laying down the law about cleaning up and pulling her weight, but by the time she'd had a shower and changed her clothes. Sonia was already cooking the dinner, and Vicky decided she'd wait for a bit before sorting things out with her. A few hours later, though, she wished that she'd had that chat with Sonia first off, because after Juliet had been put to bed, Willie came into Vicky's room while she was on the phone and told her that he was off out down the road and could she keep an eye on the baby for a short while, she was already asleep, no problem. Vicky told Jill she'd ring back and put the phone down.

'Where's Sonia?' she asked.

'She's gone to look for a place with Byron,' Willie said. But there was something shifty about his look, and Vicky guessed that they'd gone down the pub, or dancing or whatever it was they did at their age in that area. If her guess was right Willie was going to join them. She gave him a nasty look, but at the same time she was relenting at the sight of his stricken face. Poor Willie, she thought, it's not his fault.

'All right,' she said. 'But you be back here in an hour.'

As soon as Willie left, Vicky went upstairs to check on Juliet, drawn by a curiosity whose intensity she couldn't explain. She hadn't had a good look at the child before, and now she hung over the cradle, grabbed by a feeling of wonder at the strange perfection of her miniature limbs, her intricately carved fingers and her beautiful gleaming toenails. There was something fascinating, too, about the colour of her skin, a translucent and very pale beige, with a pink flush of blood showing through the places where it stretched tight over her flesh; and framing her face a mass of light brown curls, a few strands sticking damply to her forehead.

Vicky didn't know how long she stood there, suppressing the desire to reach out and touch the child, but eventually she turned away and went back down to her room. Looking at Juliet had given her a feeling of being pierced through and through with sadness, and though she tried to get back to reading the book in front of her she couldn't concentrate. In the end, although she'd told herself that she wouldn't do this, she started on a series of cleaning up jobs, moving from room to room, picking things up, drying up the dishes stacked by the sink, putting pots and pans neatly away in the cupboard. By the time she'd finished it was nearly midnight, and her lodgers hadn't yet returned. Vicky considered going to bed, but by then she was so angry that she decided to wait up and confront Sonia as soon as she returned.

It seemed a long time after that she heard the key in the door, followed by the crashing sounds of the three friends trying to enter cautiously. She gave them a little while, then went to the door of the sitting-room. The telly was switched on to one of the interminable pop programmes which seemed to be running during the middle of the night every night, and Sonia was sprawled on the sofa, while the two boys lay on the floor. They all seemed to be giggling, at nothing. It crossed Vicky's mind that she was in the position of a mother with three more or less delinquent teenagers on her hands. But she dismissed the thought immediately. She had no intention of showing the tolerance she assumed a mother would have.

'I don't care,' she said curtly, 'what time you come in or what you have been doing. It's none of my concern, as long as Willie is not getting into any trouble for which I might have to go to court and answer. What I object to is you're leaving that baby upstairs all night without making any sensible arrangments. Sonia,' Vicky continued, warming up and within a touch of getting quite carried away, 'you're a mother and you ought to be more responsible. You don't even know the first thing about me or what goes on in this house. How could you simply leave the baby, go out, and not come back for this long?'

Sonia's face switched from suppressed hilarity to a mask of dumb and sullen resentment, as if a button had been pressed.

'I left her with Willie,' Sonia muttered.

'And Willie left her with the nearest person,' Vicky said, 'which happened to be me, swearing that he'd be back in an hour's time. As it happens I didn't really mind but you must never do that again while you're here. I have no intention whatsoever of baby-sitting for you as well as putting a roof over your head, and if this goes on Juliet would probably be better off in care, and that's exactly where she'll end up.'

When Vicky knew Sonia better, she reflected that this last had been an unnecessarily cruel thing to say, but she was angry and also genuinely concerned about what seemed like Sonia's carelessness. In fact Sonia, by her own lights, was a caring and watchful mother, but Vicky, as she told herself while stomping up the stairs, wasn't to know what kind of mother the girl was, and in any case if she didn't lay down the law Willie's friends would soon be trampling all over her. At that moment Vicky was sure that what she'd said was right and not at all excessive, but days later, talking over what had happened that evening with Willie, she reflected that, if only she'd known the effect that her words would have, she might have kept her mouth firmly shut.

Chapter 7

Vicky's parting shot had left Sonia in a state which was close to terror, and that night she had practically no sleep, thinking about the possibility of her baby being taken away, and feeling as if she had wandered into a trap.

Next morning she stayed in bed late, hiding in her room until Vicky had gone, then she hurried across to Willie's room where Byron still lay on the carpet, wrapped in the sleeping-bag Vicky had lent him, and snoring his head off.

'Byron,' she said, urgently. 'Wake up, Byron. We've got to do something.'

It took her a while to get Byron awake and it wasn't until he'd had two cups of tea, and a bowl of cornflakes, that she was able to get him to pay attention to what she was saying.

'What are you talking about?' Byron asked. 'We're all right here for a bit, ain't we?'

This was a reaction which nearly drove Sonia up the wall, spurred as she was by anxiety about Juliet, and about what might happen if Vicky started carrying on like a social worker, the way they always did, and getting some authority to check up on her and the baby. Sonia had no idea what they could do, or what they could find out that would be against her, or whether she was doing anything wrong, apart from leaving her with Vicky the night before. But if she knew anything it was that the authorities, especially social workers, social security, and that, had a total and absolute power to do what they pleased about people like herself. She also knew that someone like Vicky, who was in the right kind of job and knew the right kind of people, and who behaved as if she was born telling people what to do, could probably make it happen, if for some reason she wished to punish Sonia by taking Juliet away. For all she knew she had done the wrong things and would probably be liable to various kinds of penalties if she was so unlucky as to come to the attention of anyone with the power to do something about it. All this was exactly what Sonia's experience had taught her about the world.

Byron tried to reassure her.

'That Vicky is only a hard-faced bitch of a wanker,' he said comfortingly, 'and she didn't mean it anyway.'

But the truth was that he really didn't know what Vicky meant or what she could do, or what Sonia's rights were, and even though he tried to be convincing, Sonia spotted his uncertainty, which increased her own anxiety considerably.

For the next couple of hours they sat round the table, discussing what to do, and how to make sure that Vicky didn't cause the kind of trouble she had threatened. One thing was glaringly obvious, that they couldn't just bunk down there as long as they liked. Byron might have got away with it on his own, but the addition of Sonia and the baby made their position a little more difficult. The best solution, Sonia said eventually, was for the two of them to piss off out of it and get their own flat. But the fact that neither of them had any money at all meant that they'd have to find another squat, and by now Sonia had talked herself into such a state of paranoia that she thought that finding a squat with Juliet on her hands, even if it was successful and a nice place, might render her liable to some future persecution by someone like Vicky, if not Vicky herself.

'Course what we need,' Byron said, 'is a load of money.

Then we could clear off and do the business. Find our own place. Couldn't touch you or Juliet then.'

Although he didn't say so, he was also thinking about Hyacinth. It was then that Sonia had her bright idea.

'You know that geezer I was telling you about,' Sonia said. 'The betting shop.'

'What about him?'

'We could rob him,' Sonia said. 'You've done it before.'

The room went very quiet. This was actually the very last thing that Byron had expected Sonia to say, or to be thinking. He didn't think of himself as a robber anyway. He'd been unlucky, that was all. But now Sonia had let the idea out of its cage, he suddenly started wondering about how easy or how hard it would be and about how much they could make that way.

'You don't know,' he said, 'what you're talking about. Most of them geezers who do this, you know, going round robbing people and that, they've kind of grown up in it, like they start robbing cars or breaking into meters and things like that when they're about ten years old. The rest of them if you're not like trained, it's really hard getting into it. It's like you start shaking, your knees start knocking, like you're practically shitting yourself at first. It's not easy. First thing you have to do is make them believe that you're really a nutter, like if you're threatening them, you're really going to do it, otherwise they start grabbing you or screaming or making themselves a nuisance, and then you either have to run off or really do them. I could do that, if I was with other blokes who were really hard, but not with you. Forget about it. It wouldn't work.'

'That's not what I mean,' Sonia told him. 'What I had in mind is something different.'

What had come into Sonia's mind was something she'd seen on the telly only a week before. A bunch of robbers had gone to a bank manager's house, held his family hostage, taken him into work and cleared out the safe. They'd got away with it, and Sonia's mind had flashed out a version of the same robbery, only with George Crooks in the role of victim. At that same moment she had a fantasy of herself holding a gun on George as he knelt before her begging and pleading for mercy. She smiled at Byron, and began to describe her idea.

'Wait a minute,' Byron said sceptically, as she began her spiel, 'wait a minute. Bookies don't get that much money in anyway. I mean what is it, a few thousand quid? You can't make much out of that.'

'No, no, no. You don't know what you're on about,' Sonia protested. 'The whole point is you've got to pick the right day and the right way.'

She explained. Most of the time the bookie shop where she worked didn't take in much more than a few grand a day, that was true. That was the reason bookies were always trying to expand the time they could stay open. But there were occasions when the amount of money going through the shops soared to near astronomical levels. The day of the Gold Cup every little old lady with a few bob came in to plank it on a loser. Office workers had sweepstakes which they would come in the morning and put on, small punters gambled big. Big gamblers went right round the bend. By the end of the day there could be several thousand quid sloshing around in any shop. On top of that, because of the sheer volume of work and money, some of the bookies never paid out on the big races till the next day. On a day like that there would certainly be a few grand and more in the shop.

'So how come,' Byron asked, 'them geezers don't do all the bookies on the day of the big races? I mean, that's when they'd walk in there with guns and pickaxe handles and that and grab the lot if it was that easy.'

'Well, it's not that easy is it? That's the kind of day when the shop's packed. You'd have to deal with over a dozen people any place you go, and it's not that easy. The kind of blokes who might do it would have to be anything like six of them to make sure they got away, then you'd had to split the money six ways. It's just not worth it, you might as well rob a bank.'

'So how do you reckon two of us doing all that?'

Byron thought it was a rubbish idea, but actually, he was intrigued.

'I never said,' Sonia told him, 'that we could do it that way. Did I? It would need more than the two of us. But if we could get the manager cooperating with us we could do it easy. Just pick the right day.'

'Oh yes,' Byron said, 'I suppose the manager's just going to say I fancy you Sonia here's twenty grand thank you very much.'

'Oh bollocks,' Sonia exploded. 'He's got a family, hasn't he? That's how we do it.'

Sonia had never met George's wife and daughter but she had heard a lot about them and when she thought about it there was a kind of neatness about the idea of using George's family against him which pleased her.

'I don't know,' Byron said slowly. 'Going in somewhere and knocking off a few bob is different. You're talking about kidnapping and all the rest of it. That's serious.'

'Only if it goes wrong,' Sonia said. 'What you talking about anyway? Think about it. Unless you get a job soon you're going to start doing something dodgy and now you've been inside they'll probably get you in two minutes if you start doing jobs with some of those geezers that you know. Even if you get a job, what's it going to be? Some crap like I've been doing and sooner or later you'll start doing something dodgy. And on top of that the sort of stuff that you'll be doing will only bring you in a few quid anyway. When you add it up it's a lot less risky pulling a big job and getting off somewhere else rather than hanging about and getting known and messing about breaking into houses and cars and that until they get you. Put it another way, you don't have nothing to lose.'

Byron considered it. As soon as she'd said this he'd known that she was right. Most of the men with whom he'd been banged up had been on the fiddle one way or the other for years, never made any money out of it and were spending longer and longer terms inside. When Sonia said what she did, he had a depressing picture of himself going on and on, running into people like Biggy in one nick or another and winding up a little bent old man with false teeth crouched in the corner of a cell.

'We could get a flat,' Sonia continued, 'and we'd have enough to get us some time to set up proper jobs or at least check out some way of getting on that would take the pressure off.'

'What about you?' Byron asked. 'If anything happens you'll lose your baby. You know that, don't you?'

'If I go on like this,' Sonia said, 'I'll probably lose her anyway.'

This was the truth that had been bobbing around in the back of her mind ever since Vicky had had a go at her the night before. Sonia too had found herself spinning a depressing picture of her possible future. While she was working at George's shop she'd been chatted up by several punters. A couple of them had offered her money, and at the time she hadn't been much tempted. Now she was almost sure that she would take any reasonable offer just for the sake of earning a few legitimate quid. On the other hand the idea filled her with a sort of terror. She couldn't remember her mother clearly but what she remembered was that years back on her second day in one of the schools they went to, a big girl had taunted her in the playground with the information that her mother was a prostitute. At the time she knew that it wasn't true, that there was no way that this girl could know anything about her mother or about her, except that she was a kid in care, and living in a foster-home.

Sonia had smashed her in the face and left her with a bloody nose and two black eyes, but she still had the uneasy feeling that there was every chance that her mother, who had left her crying in the back row of seats in the nave of Liverpool Cathedral, had been a woman who spent her life on the street corners. She'd had any number of fantasies, some of them invented, some of them a copy of other girls' stories, about her mother being a beautiful young heiress, who would one day trace her and come to claim her, but now she was grown up and knew more about the world, she thought on balance that the most likely thing was that her real mum had been a desperate teenager, much like she was herself. I'll never be like that, she swore to herself, the way she did practically every day when she thought about it.

Byron didn't really need much more persuasion. The problem that engaged them in argument, however, was whether to bring Willie in on what they planned to do. Willie was too young, Byron argued, swayed by some feeling of protectiveness which he always seemed to have had about Willie. Sonia didn't agree. Willie had grown up a lot. After all, he was shagging a grown woman, and doing a job, more or less supporting himself, which was better than they could do. Besides, as they knew, Willie might be young, but he was smart, with a keen brain which understood computer games and football tactics, things like that, which was more than the rest of them had ever been able to do, and if Willie had stopped in school he might have got his GCSEs and A levels no trouble. He was good at that kind of thing. So if anything, they needed someone like Willie to think about the idea and sort out the problems.

‘Anyway,’ Sonia said, ‘if we’re going to do it, how can we keep it quiet from Willie? We need to stop here for a bit till we get some money.’

It was obvious that for this purpose they needed Willie’s full cooperation, and if they started blanking him out things might turn awkward. So they agreed, Willie was in.

‘But only if he wants to be,’ Byron said virtuously. ‘I don’t want to influence Willie.’

Sonia rolled her eyes upwards. She knew, even if Byron pretended not to, that Willie, in his heart, was still El Segundo, and that he would go wherever Byron led.

‘What about the triplets?’ Byron asked.

Sonia screwed her face up. She’d forgotten about the triplets, and as soon as Byron mentioned them she felt a kind of superstitious chill, as if the mere mention of their names changed things, and made the idea serious, suddenly looming up grim and menacing like a dark wall behind which lurked some unknown threat. Not that she thought of the triplets like that. They used to get on her nerves and she didn’t feel close to them like she did with Byron and Willie, but she could remember lots of times when they’d been nice to her, and the fact that she lived with the triplets had sometimes given her a kind of immunity in the playground. The only thing was that she had always been a bit scared of them, and looking back she realized that more than once they had scared her a lot more than she ever bothered to remember. For example, the time that the park-keeper’s Alsatian bit Louis. It had been in the middle of the holidays, and the old park-keeper had died just before school broke up that year. The new one the council hired had put new locks on the sheds, and fixed the doors and gates to make it harder to get in, which irritated the triplets, because they looked on the park and all its fixtures and fittings as more or less their property, seeing that they’d spent most of their lives breaking into it. The result was a spate of break-ins and vandalism which so upset the new park-keeper that he got himself an Alsatian, with which he made random patrols at night. During one of these patrols the dog had caught the triplets leaving the hut. They ran for the railings and swung over, but not before the Alsatian's teeth had slashed Louis round the thigh, aiming for the bollocks, Louis said, laughing, the way that they trained these German attack dogs during the time of the Nazis. The thought seemed to amuse the triplets more than anything else, but it was less than a week later than someone lured the dog into the park-keeper's hut, shut him in, and set the place alight with a couple of gallon cans of petrol. It was a big item in the local newspaper. They said that the dog howled like a lost soul, that was the phrase the reporters got from one of the people who lived nearby and had heard the animal's final agony. The report concluded that the vandals hadn't realized that the dog had been shut in, a passage which the triplets pointed out to each other with faces of ostentatious sympathy for the poor dumb beast's sufferings.

'But you never know,' Mohammed told Byron in loud and self-righteous tones. 'Some of these bastards round here. I just bet they knew the poor doggie was there all the time. I just bet they knew. Don't you reckon, boys?'

The boys all agreed, the same false expression of sympathy on their faces. Then Mohammed had laughed, and they all grinned at each other, and then Sonia had known, the understanding coming to her in a shivering flash, that they were the ones who'd done it. Within a few weeks some of the kids started making out that you could hear the dog howling on dark nights, and the triplets, who were fascinated by the story, maintained, after a while, that they had also heard the ghostly howling. But unlike the other kids, it didn't seem to put them off the park, and as soon as the council built a new hut, they started breaking into that one too. From that time Sonia had reckoned that they were a bit mad. Everybody else knew that about them, and she had a vague feeling that if the triplets were involved in anything, the threat of violence wouldn't be far away. Then she thought about George and what they would have to do, and she shrugged her shoulders in resignation.

'All right,' Sonia said, 'let's have the triplets.'

Chapter 8

It was gone eight by the time Byron got off the train at Piccadilly. He had expected to feel apprehensive or emotional or some other thing, considering what had happened to him the last time he was in Manchester, but he felt very little of the kind, only a sort of excited worry about what he would say to the triplets, and how they would take it. He wasn't worried about Ray, who was kind of happy-go-lucky and good-natured, even at the worst of times, and Louis, who was different, a bit of a mean bastard, had been his closest friend at one point. It was Mohammed who worried him. Mohammed was the smartest of the lot and by a long way the most vicious of the triplets. Back when they first met Byron hadn't been able to distinguish their different characteristics, partly because they hardly talked to anyone, except among themselves, and sometimes when they were having a conversation with you they even addressed their remarks to each other, so that you had to guess what was meant for you and what was meant for one of the brothers. Their other irritating habit was that they often talked in snatches of poetry, of one kind or another. Byron had guessed, like everyone else, that their peculiarities were all to do with them being triplets, but somehow the brothers could be so weird, when they felt like it, that a lot of people they'd known had an almost superstitious feeling about them. Apart from anything else they liked to play tricks on people. If you saw them together walking down the road, it was obvious that they looked very different from each other. But if you saw each one of the three at different times you could imagine that you were seeing the same person; and that was weird too.

At school the teachers always split them into different classes, because together they were nearly always uncommunicative or troublesome, and a feature of their mischief was that it usually had a quality of sly cruelty about it. That was Mohammed's contribution, Byron thought. Thinking back, he remembered that one of the tricks the triplets had played, probably several times, was the thing that happened when Ray, who was the most extrovert and outgoing, had got off with Megan Jones, a thirteen-year-old whose parents had recently moved from Cardiff, and who a short time after appearing in their classroom had got the reputation of being a bit of a scrubber. Ray had enticed Megan to join him in the park-keeper's hut, which the brothers broke into when they felt like it, and after he had shagged her he went outside, apparently returning in a minute. But that was Louis, who was followed by Mohammed. According to Ray they had kept going in and out for hours, until Megan decided that she had to get home. This was actually the brothers' first time on the job, and luckily Megan was so inexperienced herself that she didn't work it out until the next day when she saw the brothers together and they told her how much they had enjoyed going out with her the night before.

Trouble was that when he'd found out about the triplets' background, as he had done early on, crouched on the stairs one night listening to the foster-mother on the telephone, you almost expected them to be nuts. They had been born to a married couple and lavishly looked after for the first few years of their lives, unlike Byron, who'd been dumped on the doorstep of a hospital in Sheffield, a note with his name, Byron Desire (pronounced DAYZEER, the note said) pinned to his little vest. This story was typical of most of the kids in the home where Byron lived when he met the triplets. But when he found out how the brothers had got there Byron reckoned that he and the other abandoned kids had been lucky in comparison.

The triplets' father was a Jamaican who worked as a security man. This meant that he did a lot of night work, but returning unexpectedly to the large council house the triplets' births had earned their parents, he surprised a man whom he knew slightly, climbing trouserless through the first-floor bedroom window. Calmly their father had gone to the cupboard under the sink where he kept his machete, walked back to the bedroom with it swinging in his hand, and then proceeded to slash their mother several times about the head and body until her blonde hair and smooth white body were streaming with blood, and she was dead. The triplets, standing wide-eyed in the doorway, crying and screaming, witnessed the entire act, and shrank out of the way as their father went back past them walking steadily, like a man in a dream. He went out of the door, shutting it carefully behind him, got into his car, drove out to the flyover near the big GUS neon sign, turned the wheel and took the car over the drop into the streets below. The car burst into flames, so that no one ever knew whether he had died in the crash or in the subsequent fire. After this, the triplets, who had been the pampered darlings of local advertisers, baby-food and baby-clothes and baby-care firms, were put into care, and then up for adoption. But for some reason no one seemed to want to adopt three fucked-up, sullen and mixed-up mixed-race triplets. In fact the triplets were never irrational or even particularly wild. What was frightening about them later on was the directness and economy with which they expressed their desires and the physical force they could bring to bear in fulfilling them.

Byron was looking forward to seeing them, because although they scared him a little, like they scared everyone who knew them well, the triplets had been a routine part of his life for a long time while he grew up, and he often thought about them and, in a funny way, missed them. He was one of the few people, in fact, who knew themselves to be in the triplets' permanent good books, because one time, early on, he had saved Louis from a serious beating in the playground. Even back then the triplets were well known to be hard, and bigger kids left them alone. But on this occasion Louis had been waiting for Mohammed and Ray, who had been kept in, to emerge from the school building. A little gang of older boys had started, the way they did, having a go, and Louis, who like all the triplets had no more sense of personal danger than your average Rottweiler, had steamed straight in after they called him a half-caste nigger bastard. It was a moderate enough insult for the place and the time, but Louis took it badly. When Byron turned up, the fight was nearly over. Louis was being held round the throat by one of the boys while the others delivered a series of well-aimed kicks to his lower half. Byron hadn't thought about it, not more than the merest zillionth of a second anyway. He had thrown his cycle bag with his football boots in it at the head of one of the assailants and jumped straight in, delivering a satisfactory karate kick to the kidneys of the boy who was holding Louis. The white boys had reckoned on beating up one kid, rather than fighting with two, even if they were quite small, and they scattered as soon as they realized that another contestant was also in the ring. In a moment they were gone, while Louis and Byron ended up clinging to the railings, grinning at each other.

After that Byron was in solid with the triplets. What he had done was actually their most reliable measure, maybe their only measure, of friendship or goodwill, and it earned him their triple loyalty. You had to go a long way before the brothers trusted you or treated you like a friend, but if you did something for one of them it was as if you had done it for all three. There was more to it. After Byron had been hanging out with the brothers for a bit a strange thing began to happen. It was as if he too could read what was in their minds at any one time. They'd be walking down the pavement and see another kid, and all of a sudden they'd all feel suspicious or curious at the same time, and like some miracle Byron could sense himself getting the same feeling. Or they'd be coming out of the cinema, and they'd all walk towards a hamburger joint without a word, and without thinking about it, they'd all order exactly the same meal at the same time. That was what it was like being with the triplets. When you were in, you were in.

So Byron knew that the brothers used to trust him, and for that reason they'd hold still long enough to talk to him. After that he couldn't be certain. The first problem, though, was finding them. He knew they were around Moss Side somewhere. That's where they'd been all along, ever since they'd been released from care, but he didn't know exactly where, and as he walked down Oxford Road towards Moss Lane he was casting around for alternative ways of locating them. In the end he went into a pub near Alexandra Park gates, which was the middle of the district, and asked the man behind the bar whether he knew the triplets. The barman was young and black, about Byron's age, with a gleaming shaved head and a small neat moustache. He gave Byron a suspicious look and shook his head.

'Don't know,' he said. 'Don't know them.'

Byron was sure that this was a lie, but in the circumstances there was nothing he could do about it, so he pushed on to the next pub down the road and asked again, getting the same reply. After he'd asked in half a dozen places, he'd begun to get the idea that no one would admit to a stranger that they knew the triplets and he'd have to find another way of locating them. That was when his luck changed. He decided to have a beer in a place down Princess Road where he used to go regularly, and he'd just walked in when he saw what looked, for a moment, like a vision. Black Valentino suit, a canary yellow waistcoat with a black stripe and a yellow silk tie with a black diamond-shape pattern. He looked away almost immediately because he guessed that a man dressed so conspicuously would resent being stared at, but he'd only taken a few steps towards the bar when he heard a voice calling his name. Byron turned round, recognizing the sound of the voice, even before he saw who it was. The face above the waistcoat was brown, only a shade darker than his, and it was split by a huge grin in the middle of which gleamed a pure gold tooth. Vincent.

They'd met in the Scrubs, where Vincent had been serving time for immoral earnings, but his sentence had been fairly short and they were mere acquaintances. At the same time Byron guessed that if Vincent knew anything about the triplets, he would tell him. He gave Vincent a greeting with his closed fist, and Vincent took his right arm from round one of the two blondes who were cuddling up next to him and reached out to touch his fist against Byron's.

Byron knew better than to ask his question straight away, however, and they talked for a few minutes about mutual acquaintances before he mentioned the triplets to Vince.

'Don't know them guys really,' Vince said. 'They bad, you know.'

Byron nodded, and told Vince that he'd grown up with the triplets and he wanted to say hello to them.

'They come by here sometimes,' Vincent said, 'but I don't see them lately. I hear they had a little trouble, but I don't know for sure.'

Byron didn't ask what the trouble was. He imagined

that he'd find out soon enough, but after Vincent had racked his brains for a while he made a guess that the brothers lived on the west end of Moss Lane near Whalley Range. Then he snapped his fingers.

'I saw them in a shop down there just close by the junction. Right there where Withington Road cuts across.'

He couldn't be more precise, but as Byron turned to go Vince disentangled himself from the blondes and came closer to him.

'If you really want to find them,' he said, 'check some of them young boys dealing down by the park. All of them get their supplies from those guys, and I didn't tell you that.'

Byron went straight on down Moss Lane when he left the pub. He had a feeling that he'd get nowhere asking one of the young dealers and, in any case, he'd almost reached the shop before one of them approached him. He was an anxious-looking boy in an anorak.

'Rock? Rock? You want rock?'

Byron shook his head, then he remembered Vincent's words.

'Hey,' he said quickly, 'you know where the triplets live?'

The boy's expression turned even more anxious, and he shook his head and walked away. Byron had more or less expected this and he continued into the shop, where the Asian man behind the counter frowned when he asked his question and shook his head vigorously.

'No,' he said. 'Don't know.'

After this Byron didn't know quite what to do. He began walking back along Moss Lane thinking about various possibilities. He could look in the telephone book, although he suspected that their names wouldn't be there. He could check the voters' register at the library in the morning. Then he thought of going up to the flat and asking Marie. Perhaps he could telephone, he thought, but only as a last resort. The idea of facing Fergus again made his stomach churn. Automatically, he had strayed off the road and begun walking through the courtyard that led towards the tower where he used to live, and out of which he had departed so suddenly a few days ago. Suddenly from behind a pillar to his left he heard a slight noise, like a shoe scraping on the ground, followed by a hiss. He looked round. The path past the bottom of the tower was lighted but the lamps threw peculiar shadows and the couldn't be sure whether there was someone lurking there. He turned to face whatever it was that was coming up behind him.

'If I should meet thee,' a voice said, 'after long years, how should I greet thee?'

'Louis,' Byron said. 'Is that you, Louis?'

Louis stepped out from behind a pillar, grinning.

'Lord Byron,' Louis said.

They shook hands and hugged each other with real feeling.

Byron had forgotten how big the triplets were. He was only a fraction of an inch shorter than six feet but Louis stood a few inches taller, and since Byron had last seen him he seemed to have got broader. His hair was growing in a round pad on top of his head which made him look even more of a giant.

'I heard,' Louis said, 'that some wanker was wandering round here looking for us. I followed you all down Moss Lane laughing.'

Byron wondered for a moment why he hadn't simply come out and said hello instead of fooling around, but he knew now that was how the brothers did things and he didn't bother asking.

'Let's go see the boys,' Louis said.

The house Louis led Byron to was on the other side of Withington Road, round the back, where there were still some of the big houses which, as Louis told him, the rich businessmen of the city used to live in. The house had that big, old look which made him think that rich old people must live there, but inside he sensed the presence of the triplets at once. In the room at the front which had big bay windows and stretched out to French windows at the back, Mohammed and Ray were sitting watching television. In another corner of the room a CD player was going full blast, and when Byron looked a bit more closely he realized that Ray was playing a computer game with a monitor which he was holding in his lap. None of this actually surprised Byron. The triplets had always conducted several different activities in the same space at the same time, and he could never work out, for instance, which one was actually watching the television, and which one was listening to the music, or doing whatever else was going on. Sometimes this used to cause ferocious arguments between them, and Byron used to wonder why at least one of them didn't take themselves to another room instead of rowing about the fact that they were disturbing each other. But this kind of solution never seemed to occur to the triplets.

'Byron,' Mohammed shouted, 'bloody Byron.'

'Byron,' Ray shouted next, 'it's Byron.'

'It's Byron, isn't it?' Louis said in his turn. 'It was him going round asking about us.'

Byron sat down when the greetings were over and began answering their questions, about where he'd been, and what had been happening to him. It was more difficult than he remembered speaking to all three of them at once because they would ask variants on the same question almost at the same time and before he'd finished answering they'd be asking him something else. It was like being in a room with three manic interrogators.

Near him, against the wall, was a long shallow cabinet, about five feet high, with a glass front and glass shelves.

On the shelves were various objects, carefully displayed. Byron recognized the boxing trophies the triplets had won at school, before they had got bored with the idea and given it up. On the bottom shelf was a wig, and a pair of women's panties.

'Souvenirs,' Mohammed said, following the direction of Byron's eyes.

'Wait a minute,' Louis said before Byron could ask about the things in the cabinet. 'You want some food? We're having dinner late tonight.'

'See?' Mohammed said. 'We must have known you were coming.'

'Bollocks,' Byron replied amiably. 'Don't try your tricks on me.'

He knew this was one of Mohammed's tactics. The triplets had discovered early on that something about them provoked a superstitious feeling in some people, and it was one of the things they'd played on since Byron had first known them.

The triplets grinned with the same mocking air.

'All right,' Mohammed said. 'You're too clever for us. Ray's woman hasn't turned up yet, so we have to wait.'

'Who's cooking then?' Bryon asked. 'Not you lot, because if you are I'll nip out and get some chips.'

None of the triplets had ever bothered to learn how to boil an egg in all the time that Byron had known them, and he imagined that they hadn't changed.

'Don't worry,' Louis said, 'it'll be OK.'

The doorbell rang, and Ray got up and went out.

'We heard you got done,' Mohammed said.

Byron nodded.

'Dreadful, man,' Louis said. 'You should have stopped here with us.'

Ray came back into the room followed by a tall blonde girl with a foreign look about her. He introduced her to Byron, who didn't quite catch her name and didn't have the chance to ask because Mohammed got up immediately and said, 'Come on then, come on then.' But his eagerness was deceptive, because as he got up he bent sideways, clutched at his leg and leaned on the back of the sofa with the other hand before he straightened up and limped towards the door. It was on the tip of Byron's tongue to ask what was wrong with the leg, but none of the brothers had remarked on it, or shown any sign of noticing Mohammed's difficulty, so Byron kept his mouth shut.

Shuffling behind Mohammed he followed them across the hallway into the room opposite, then stopped short, startled by the sight of two more blonde girls who in that instant looked like exact copies of the one he had just seen. He felt the triplets watching him and suddenly they all began laughing.

'All right,' Byron said, 'you three aren't sisters, are you?'

That made them all laugh even harder.

'No,' Louis said, 'you twat, they don't even look alike.'

At this the triplets practically screamed with laughter. Eventually they recovered enough to tell Byron that the girls were all from different countries for a start. Helga was German, Brite was Norwegian and Anna was from Poland. It was coincidence, Louis said, that they were all blonde, a statement which Byron took with a pinch of salt. But when they sat down to the dinner which had been cooked by Brite and Anna, and Byron had a good look at them close up, he realized that they didn't look alike at all. The resemblance was on the surface; the colour of their hair, their short skirts and long legs, their height, all these things combined to give the illusion. Later on he learnt that they were all students, but that too was deceptive. Brite was a nurse on some kind of exchange, Helga studied engineering at the university and Anna was a hairdressing apprentice.

'See how different they are?' Mohammed said, grinning.

Byron agreed, but at the same time he couldn't help noticing that the three girls seemed to have already taken on all the triplets' mannerisms. They grinned and laughed almost in the same second as the triplets did, and when one of the boys reached out for a dish, one of the girls always seemed to have her hand already outstretched to pass it to him. Equally, they let Mohammed do the talking and although they answered Byron's questions about where they came from and what they did in a sociable enough way, they confined themselves to replying, and did nothing at all to start up any conversational lines. This didn't surprise Byron too much. What surprised him was that they seemed to be a long way from the kind of women who usually hung out with boys he knew. They were foreign to begin with, but that didn't matter so much. What struck him was the fact that as they talked, they mentioned their parents and schools and dropped hints about their careers, all of which, in the world where Byron and the triplets had grown up, were things even more foreign than Norway or Poland or bloody Timbuctoo. Somehow he had a suspicion that the brothers knew what he was thinking, because he caught them more than once, while he was speaking to one of the girls, watching him with a sly, ironic smile on their three faces, and he guessed that the whole evening was a chance for them to show off their new life, which included the beautiful foreign girls, in the very same way that they used to show off every feature of their new toys and games. For their twelfth birthday they'd got a BMX bike from some forgotten relative and they'd spent hours describing its properties to the other kids, but whenever anyone else asked if they could ride it, the triplets had only one answer, all speaking at the same time, right off – 'No'.

But when he thought about it, it didn't surprise him so much that the triplets could acquire women like the foreign girls round the table. They'd always attracted girls, right from the beginning when they had pulled Megan, and then, once they'd learnt what they could do, they'd pulled most of the other girls in the class, with an ease that excited Byron's envy and admiration. That was the way they always were. But what now puzzled Byron, and made him curious, even mystified, was how much the triplets' behaviour seemed to have changed. Some things were still the same. For instance, one of them would say what they thought or felt, as if they were a group with an appointed spokesman, which in a way he supposed they were. Tonight it appeared to be Mohammed doing the talking. But there was something different about them, an air of relaxation, as if they were totally in control of everything round them.

Their mood had the same effect on Byron, and as the evening progressed he felt himself relaxing into the kind of nostalgic warmth he had with Sonia and Willie. The triplets had asked about the other two, of course, and he'd told them at length about Sonia's job, which made them screech with laughter, and then he told them about Willie and Vicky which made them laugh even harder. By the end of the meal Byron had almost forgotten why he was there.

When it had crossed his mind he'd wondered how he would raise the subject, because he couldn't speak in front of the women, and in any case, he was beginning to doubt that the triplets would go for his scam. So it was a bit of shock, as if the time had come to take an exam for which he wasn't ready, when Mohammed pushed himself carefully away from the table, and stood up.

'Let's go,' Mohammed said. 'We've got some things to do, and you've got some things you want to tell us. Right?'

Byron couldn't see whether some kind of signal had passed between them, but the brothers were all standing, the women had already begun clearing the table, and they walked back into the next room in complete silence.

Chapter 9

'Waste of time,' Mohammed said. His tone was casual, but in the circumstances it probably represented a firm collective decision.

Byron had put the case as strongly as he could, but at the end of his pitch, he had the sense that the triplets were losing interest.

'Come on,' Byron said, 'you could get away with a few grand each just for a day trip down to London.'

'We're doing all right here,' Mohammed said.

The same thought had been in Byron's mind, especially when he thought about Brite, Helga and Anna. He'd asked the triplets which ones were their particular women and the brothers had responded by giving each other a sly grin.

'Doesn't matter,' Mohammed had said. 'We've all been out with each other from time to time. We're brothers you know. Share and share alike.'

At that point Byron knew how difficult it was going to be persuading the brothers.

'On top of that,' Mohammed said, 'we don't fancy getting banged up, you know what I mean? It's not worth it.'

'That patch of blue we prisoners call the sky,' Ray said. 'Don't fancy it.'

'I know what you mean,' Byron said, 'but it's not like that at all. Number one we ain't walking into some place and lashing people down or holding a gun on them. This is straightforward. I told you Sonia knows the bloke. She's got it all sussed, and we'll do the dodgy bits. No one should even see your face. This is going to be easy, man.'

The brothers looked sceptical and Byron thought again.

'What's happened to your leg?' he asked Mohammed.

The brothers scowled.

'Bit of trouble. That's all,' Mohammed said.

'What? Some geezer had a go. Right?' Byron charged. 'Am I right?'

'We sorted it,' Louis said. 'Every little git nowadays that can get his hands on a gun reckons to be cheeky, but it's no problem.'

'Gunshot, was it?' Byron asked.

Mohammed nodded, the scowl still on his face.

'That's just what I mean,' Byron said. 'It's all down to you, this lot. Tonight I was going round asking for you and nobody would tell me anything, like people just up the road were making out they never heard of you. You know what that means don't you? Everybody knows what you're doing, who you are, and where you are, and what have you got? You're getting your dope from somewhere else, you have to pay what they tell you and then you have to split it up small and distribute to dozens of little geezers. Anyone of them can shop you. You're like some kind of franchise manager, risking your lives all the time, without getting your hands on the real profits.'

Over dinner Byron had worked it all out, and he had the suspicion that the triplets had probably thought of and discussed everything he was saying.

'Think about it,' Byron said. 'Some other geezer is getting the real profit, while you're the middlemen. It's all right now, but what happens when some of these kids decide that they want to take over from you? Or someone else up the line gets nicked and grasses you up? Don't talk to me about what's worth it. You guys are living on a time bomb, and you know that as well as I do. What I'm offering you is a chance to make a score and maybe get enough to set up in business for yourself, get a little independence, get somebody else to go out every night and keep the kids in order. Let somebody else get their fucking leg blown off while you're getting the profits.'

For a moment, the scowl on the triplets' face had deepened. Byron knew how quickly their rage could be triggered, and just then he thought he might have gone too far. But by the time he'd finished their faces smoothed into masks of serious consideration.

'Worked all this out for yourself?' Mohammed asked.

Byron nodded, without taking his eyes away.

'You've got a point,' Mohammed said. 'But I don't reckon one job could raise the kind of money we need to go independent.'

'Unless,' Byron said, 'it wasn't like just one job. That's how I see it. If it works we can do it again somewhere else. If it's as easy as it looks and we know that it works we can clear out quite a few shops in various places. Look at the geezers that invented that trick with the bulldozers and the cash machines. Millions they knocked off, before the banks worked out what to do, and they got clean away.'

Byron had a feeling this was an exaggeration, but he reasoned it was a pardonable one in the circumstances. The triplets looked at each other.

'That makes sense,' Mohammed said slowly. 'That's different. How much d'you reckon exactly?'

Byron made a guess, based on what Sonia had told him.

'Well, if it's the day of a big race, anything between twenty-five and thirty grand.'

'There's three of us and three of you,' Mohammed said. 'We'll go halves then. Minimum fifteen grand. Anything less you owe us.'

'Fair enough,' Byron agreed. He knew that there'd be no point in arguing about it.

The difficult bit was over. The arrangements were easy to make. Louis and Ray would come down to London the night before the big race, as long as Byron gave them the word that the job was still on. As for Mohammed, he would stay to provide the boys with an alibi, in case something went wrong. As long as one of them was around no one would imagine that the other two were far away, and because most people couldn't tell them apart, all he'd have to do was appear in a few places that day to register their presence. Byron guessed that this was a routine manoeuvre, and it didn't worry him, because it would be easier having just Ray and Louis around than all three.

By the time they were all satisfied, it was round about eleven, but as Byron realized in a moment, the night was just beginning for the brothers.

'You'd better come with us then, Byron,' Louis said. 'Time to do a little business. Know what I mean?'

'Let us go, through certain half-deserted streets,' Mohammed said. 'The muttering retreats of restless nights in one-night cheap hotels.'

For the next hour or so Byron and the brothers drove back and forth through the area. After a while Byron began to recognize a pattern. For instance, they drove along Withington Road and turned left towards Alexandra Park, then Louis, who was driving, stopped and wound down the window. A boy came up and without a word handed over some money, folded in a thin wad. Louis took it, passed it over his shoulder to Mohammed, and they drove on. Sometimes the shadow at the window would be a woman, thickly made up, in a long coat, short skirt and high heels. But whoever it was they'd always pass some money over. After half a dozen such stops Ray nudged Byron as they wheeled into Wilmslow Road.

'Here,' he said, 'have you had a bit since you've been out?'

Byron shrugged. The truth was that he hadn't touched a woman except for Sonia since he'd been out, and for the last couple of days he hadn't thought of much else, when he wasn't thinking about money, but although he'd tried to pick up a couple of girls nothing much seemed to work. Sitting opposite the brothers' women that night, eyeing up their firm breasts and the smooth thighs stretching the fabric of their tight skirts, had made things worse. He thought of Katrina but it was now too late to phone her.

'That last one,' Ray said, 'how about that one? You fancy a bit?'

Byron cast his mind back. He hadn't had a good look but he retained an impression of big breasts and curly black hair. Her face can't have been that bad either or he'd have noticed.

'Don't be stupid,' Louis said. 'You can't put Byron on to that. Put it in her and the jimmy would probably corrode in thirty seconds. Dick drop right off before he could get it out. We can do Byron better than that.'

'Never mind Byron,' Mohammed said, 'let's do the business first.'

It was at this point that it struck Byron that there might be more to this expedition than a routine nightly round, or to put it another way, as he told Sonia later, the brothers' nightly round wasn't like what most people would call routine.

'We've got a lot of time,' Louis said, 'maybe half an hour. Plenty of time for Byron to dip his wick.'

'For Christ's sake,' Byron said. 'Don't worry about me.'

‘Leave off,’ Louis said. ‘You’re dying for it, you bastard.’

Byron hadn’t been sure whether or not he was, but when Louis spoke he suddenly realized that he had a tortured erection which he seemed to have been nursing for the last two years.

‘There he is,’ Louis said suddenly. ‘Got him.’

Up ahead Byron saw two men, both wearing long leather coats, walking down the pavement. The car had slowed down, and Ray opened the glove compartment and took out two pistols, one of which he handed to Louis, who put it on the dashboard in front of him.

‘What’s going on?’ Byron asked. ‘If you guys are going to have a ruck, let me out here.’

‘Fuck off, Byron,’ Louis said. ‘You’re with us.’

He speeded up.

‘I like a look of agony,’ Mohammed said, grinning at Byron, ‘because I know it’s true.’

‘Men do not sham convulsion,’ Ray shouted, ‘nor simulate a throe.’

Byron guessed it was poetry, but he wished they would shut up. Louis had come level with the men on the pavement, and pulled up with a screech of brakes. As he did so Ray, who’d already thrown open his door, leaped out and, flying across the pavement, banged into one of the leather coats and went down holding on to him. The other youth, who, when he looked around, seemed to take in the car and Louis coming round the front of the bonnet in one glance, simply turned and ran, sprinting up the road on his trainers like a supercharged Linford Christie.

‘Look at that bugger go,’ Mohammed said. ‘Don’t know what he’s running for. We’ll only get him tomorrow.’

On the pavement Louis and Ray had hauled the remaining youth to his feet and were holding him up against the boarded-up front of a shop. As Byron watched, they began hitting the boy, with a smooth and terrible fluency, like boxers, jostling shoulder to shoulder for their turn at a punchbag. The boy hadn't even tried to hit back, and it was all over in what seemed like a few seconds. The brothers stepped away from him, and the boy fell to the ground. Louis and Ray turned round, made their way back to the car, and got in.

'So what was that all about?' Byron said as the car moved off down Moss Lane.

Louis laughed.

'You don't want to know,' he said. 'We didn't hurt him. Just kind of a reminder.'

'Sorry, Byron,' Ray said. 'Now you're out you must be missing all them punch-ups you have in prison. Right? If we'd remembered we'd have give you a chance to get stuck in.'

Byron gave him two fingers, and the triplets laughed uproariously.

Louis had speeded up, slotting in to the line of traffic heading straight out of the city, as if they were driving up towards the M62.

'Where are we going now?' Byron asked.

'Wait and see,' Louis said mysteriously.

Byron noted that now Louis was doing most of the talking, and he remembered that the role of spokesman seemed to shift between the brothers according to what was happening. Now they were in action Louis seemed to have become the leader.

The traffic was light at that time of night, and before long they were speeding through a suburban district, with new houses, by the look of them, set in large gardens. Suddenly Louis turned off the dual carriageway into a wide road, with the respectable air of an established residential district. After about half a mile he turned the corner into a smaller road fringed with trees. The houses here lurked behind high hedges. Then Louis turned another corner into a narrow lane and drew up beside a six-foot wooden fence. The brothers got out, followed by Byron, Mohammed leaning, half sitting, against the bonnet of the Merc.

'What's going on?' Byron asked.

'Shush,' Mohammed said.

Ray opened the boot of the car and took out a long bundle, which he unwrapped, and Byron saw that it contained what looked like a couple of machetes and some rusty iron bars. Ray and Louis selected their implements, and walked a few yards away along the fence. Louis banged softly on the wood, then both the brothers began digging at it about knee high. Behind the fence Byron heard a low growl and a scrabbling sound and he retreated a few steps, but the sound didn't seem to worry the brothers. They had attacked the fence with such ferocious energy that in a few minutes they had created a hole which they then proceeded to enlarge with the machetes. Meanwhile the scrabbling and growling behind the fence had increased to what seemed to Byron's ears like a crescendo of furious animal rage. At this point Ray moved aside while Louis carved at the hole with what looked like comparative precision. Suddenly he jumped backwards and instanteously the head of a snarling Rottweiler emerged. At first all Byron could see was the grinning muzzle of the beast, then, with a strength and rage that was so enormous that it made the fence shake, the whole of its head pushed through, and it snapped its jaws right and left, the legs scrabbling and scratching furiously at the fence. Byron jumped backwards and opened the back door of the car, ready to jump in. But this was what the brothers were waiting for, and as the dog seemed about to spring out of the hole, Ray brought his machete down in a glittering sweep. Byron heard a yelp, and the brothers leaped backwards.

Something spurted and splashed in a huge dark fountain right across the road, splattering softly, and then gurgling over the pavement. The dog's head hit the ground with a loud thump a couple of yards away and rolled to the front of the car. Byron was standing, his hand still gripping the door of the Merc as if frozen in place. The whole thing had taken only a few minutes and he felt unreal, as if he'd wandered into a dream. The next thing he heard was a sort of roar, which in a second he realized was the sound of the triplets laughing and cheering. Louis moved forward, delicately avoiding the flood of blood at his feet, impaled the dog's head on his machete, and raising his arm catapulted it over the fence.

'Get in then,' Mohammed said to Byron. 'Unless you want to hang about and see if they've got some more dogs.'

Byron got in, and Louis, in the seat in front of him, fixed his seatbelt carefully, then switched on the engine. He looked round at Byron.

'You all right then?' Louis asked grinning.

Byron nodded his head. He couldn't speak.

'OK,' Louis said. 'Business finish. Now let's go and have a bit of a laugh.'

In what seemed only a few minutes, they were back in Moss Lane. Louis swung off to the right and half-way to the next corner he pulled over. As soon as the car stopped Byron heard the music. The building was a red brick box with a couple of lights illuminating the front. Except for the lights it looked like a very large brick shithouse.

'Come on,' Louis said. 'We're going in here.'

Byron followed Louis and Ray on to the pavement but Mohammed didn't move.

'He'll stop and wait for us,' Louis said. 'He doesn't feel like it.'

Byron wondered, for a moment, how he knew, because

Mohammed hadn't spoken, but he guessed that this too was one of the triplets' tricks.

Inside the club was crowded. Almost all the men were young and black or mixed-race. The women on the other hand were about evenly divided, about half of them white, the other half mixed-race and black. Louis and Ray led the way to the bar, which was a long trestle table in one corner of the basement. The man behind it handed them three bottles of beer without asking, and the brothers turned to look over the room, like men who were masters of all they surveyed. The noise of the music was such that conversation was impossible, but in a little while Ray nudged Byron.

'What about that one?'

The one he was indicating was a big girl. In her high heels she stood about the same height as Byron. He took a good look. Broad Irish face, reddish blonde hair which flowed down over her shoulders, a large firm bosom, and great long legs.

'Yes,' Byron said immediately.

Ray laughed and walked off across the room. The girl was dancing, smoochily wrapped up in the arms of a tall, thin black shinehead, but Ray, without hesitating, tapped him on the shoulder and said something. The shinehead looked over towards Byron and Louis, nodded, and turned away. Ray spoke to the girl, smiling broadly, and in a few seconds she stopped, picked up her bag which she slung over her shoulder, and followed him over to where Byron was standing.

Ray introduced them quickly. Her name was Maureen, he said, and she had recently moved over from Dublin. She smiled and ducked her head at Byron, without speaking.

'Dublin's fair city,' Louis shouted in Byron's ear, 'where the girls are so pretty.'

Ray was already heading for the door, followed by

Maureen. In a moment they were out on the pavement. Ray turned right, away from the Mercedes, and set off at a fast walk.

'Where are we going?' Byron asked.

The brothers laughed. Maureen paused, and dropped back next to Byron. She tucked her arm under his and leaned against him a little. Along the arm she was holding Byron could feel her big, soft tits and the sensation seemed to go right through him. The smell of her perfume felt like an electric current going straight into his brain, exciting him so much that he could hardly breathe.

'Just down the road,' Louis said.

They walked in silence down to the next corner, turned left, and a few yards further down stopped next to a black transit van. Maureen opened her bag, took out some keys, opened the sliding doors on the side, and climbed in.

'Go on then,' Ray said, pushing Byron.

Byron climbed in behind Maureen, and paused uncertainly, peering in.

'Come on then,' Maureen said from the dark interior of the van. Her voice wasn't what he'd expected. It was soft and sweet and Irish and friendly, the sound of her pushing his eagerness to an anguished peak. He stumbled forward and the doors slid shut behind him. A hand touched, felt his arm, then held and pulled him gently towards the back of the van. Suddenly he heard the front doors slam and he whipped round to see Ray and Louis climbing into the front seat of the van.

'Don't mind us,' Louis's voice said. 'We'll just sit here and wait for you.'

They giggled in unison. In other circumstances Byron might have objected, but he guessed that the brothers probably thought what they were doing was completely normal, and in any case he was now too worked up at the thought of planking Maureen to be bothered.

As his eyes became more accustomed to the darkness inside the van he realized that Maureen was now lying on the floor. She must have already pulled her skirt up round her waist, and he could see by the faint haze of reflected light through the windscreen the glowing white skin of her thighs. Byron unzipped his trousers, fumbling in his haste.

'Here,' Maureen said. She was holding out something which he realized was a condom. He took it, fingers shaking, and smoothed it on to the rigid pole in front of him.

'Go on then,' he heard Ray saying.

Byron needed no more encouragement. Immediately he went down on to his knees, and right then he could see himself as he imagined the brothers were seeing him from the front seat, kneeling between Maureen's wide open legs, the way they knelt in church in front of the altar. The idea made his cock stiffer, if that was possible, and he stared down at her, burning the sight of her body laid out before him into his memory, as if that would be his last second on earth, and savouring the knowledge that as soon as he wanted he could plunge right into her. As he hesitated, she made a movement, pushing her crotch up towards him, but suddenly it flashed across Byron's mind that he'd waited for this moment for over a year and he wasn't going to waste any of it. He reached forward and unbuttoned her sweater, then pulled her bra down over her shoulders, uncupping her breasts. They spilled out over her chest, in the darkness, awesome and enormous. He paused for a moment, looking at them with a feeling close to worship, and then touched them lightly, stroking his fingers over them, before squeezing harder and harder. Maureen made a grunting sound, stretched out her hands and held his cock between them, gripping it tight.

'Go for it, boy,' one of the brothers said, but his voice

seemed to be coming from a long way off. Byron relaxed his grip, then squeezed her breasts again, and Maureen arched her neck, throwing her head back and making her whole torso shake and quiver, then she let go his dick, put her hands on his hips and pulled him forward between her thighs. Byron went, falling forward on to her soft belly, sliding right into her without aiming, and for a moment he was astonished by the sheer heat and muscular strength of the flesh which gripped and enfolded his cock, and then he had no more time for thoughts.

Chapter 10

'I don't know,' Sonia said, 'she's sort of suspicious, you know, and while you were away she asked me if we'd got anything fixed up and when we were leaving. All that crap.'

'Don't worry,' Byron said. He had an idea about how to handle Vicky but he hadn't worked it out yet. 'We've only got a week and a little bit anyway before the race. She's not going to chuck us out before then.'

'But she's bound to notice something,' Sonia insisted. 'Suppose she goes to the cops afterwards.'

'Don't worry,' Byron said again. 'We'll sort it out.'

Sonia's fussing was getting on his nerves a little right then. They were trying to work out a plan for what to do on the day, and she'd been going on about Vicky for a good half hour.

'Let's get on,' Byron said.

They had the A-Z open at the page where George lived. Sonia knew his address. She wasn't supposed to, and he had tried to keep it hidden from her, but it had been easy to get it off one of the documents which came to him as manager, and when she'd found out about his betrayal, she'd had various fantasies about going up there and taking her revenge. So the address was one thing that was branded on her memory.

This was Enfield, a part of London neither Sonia nor Byron knew anything about, and they agreed they'd have to go up and check out the movements of George's family.

'We don't want to go up there on the day,' Byron said,

'and find it's full of blokes fixing the electricity, or like she's shagging the milkman or something.'

They reached agreement on what to do quickly and within a couple of hours they were on the tube, Sonia nursing Juliet in her lap, on the way to one of the last stations on the Piccadilly Line. Byron had thought at first that it would be better just for him to go while Sonia stayed home and looked after Juliet, but Sonia saw herself as the planner and the brains of the enterprise and she insisted that she too had, at least, to see where George lived, even though she couldn't necessarily spend as much time as Byron on surveillance. Byron had his own ideas about why she was so keen to go, but he kept them to himself.

They got off at Oakwood and took the bus to the stop opposite George's road. It was like the country out here, with trees lining the streets and narrow winding roads.

'We could get a place out here, you know,' Sonia remarked to Byron. 'It would be really good for Juliet. She'd love playing out around here.'

The thought had also occurred to her that they would have good schools, and maybe there'd be plenty of nice teenagers willing to baby-sit for practically nothing. It looked that kind of place. But when they walked down George's road the first difficulty was that there was nobody else in sight. There were lots of cars parked in the driveways, but if you stood or hung about, you'd probably be very conspicuous. Byron and Sonia, with Byron now carrying Juliet, walked slowly past George's house. It was a two-storey detached house with a crescent-shaped drive for the cars, flower-beds in front, and they guessed, a big garden with a lawn behind.

'Lovely,' Sonia muttered viciously, staring at the coloured glass panes in the door. She would have loved to have been brought up in a place like this, or even to have the chance of living there, for a while anyway.

'You'd best go back,' Byron said. 'I'll see if I can find some place to hang out and check out what's going on.'

They walked back and Sonia mooched over to the bus stop. She felt angry and sad and lethargic, all at the same time, and now she felt a bit sorry that she had come.

Byron walked back down the road, and after he'd been up and down a couple of times, he worked out that if he stood near the bus stop he could more or less see the front of George's house, and still be far enough away not to be noticed. Luckily it was still getting dark fairly early, and at night he could get closer.

At about three in the afternoon a woman in a Mini Metro, her dark hair pinned back in a pony-tail, drove up to the front of the house, parked, and went in. About an hour later three schoolgirls walked down the road, and one of them split off from the others and went into the house. Byron had seen them getting off the bus, and he hadn't noticed anything special about the girl, twelve years old in ankle socks and a black blazer with a badge on it. He waited a little longer, but he'd been there a couple of hours and he had the uneasy feeling that if he stayed much longer without moving he'd begin to attract attention. Besides, he was cold. It was spring weather, warm enough for a quick walk down the road, but it was freezing when you stood in one place out in the open for any length of time. Next time, Byron decided, he would bring gloves and a coat. In any case, he had covered the important time, and Byron wound his way back to West London with the feeling of a job well done.

Back at Vicky's house, however, there was a slight air of tension. Willie had told Vicky that Byron had gone to Manchester to sort out some private business about his daughter, and look for a job. Vicky's curiosity had been roused, and she also wanted to know how he'd got on. Byron hated having to answer these questions. To begin with, he understood that the less anyone knew about him the better off he was. It was one of the tricks that various authorities used to keep track of you and keep you under control and he had an instinctive resistance to letting Vicky know any more about himself than she had to. So he was annoyed with Vicky for asking, and answered slowly and sullenly.

'So, Byron,' Vicky had said, 'did you stay with your baby's mother in Manchester?'

Byron said no, then regretted it because Vicky continued.

'So where did you stay?'

'With some friends,' Byron told her, looking away and keeping his voice down, practically to an inaudible mutter.

Vicky got the point, and stopped asking. But after they'd had their dinner she called Willie into her study and told him that she wanted his friends gone by the weekend.

'I know it's difficult for you, Willie,' she said sympathetically. 'Do you want me to tell them?'

She felt she was treading on eggshells here with Willie. She could see that he was torn between the life he had with her and his loyalty to Byron and Sonia. But she was determined to resolve the issue, if only because she had a sense that there was something going on under the surface of the group, and she wasn't quite sure what it was. Her suspicion was that they were planning or indeed carrying out some kind of scam, and she was determined either to break Willie out of it, or if he wanted to be with them in whatever it was they were doing, to give him up and get him out of her life. The truth was that when Vicky thought sensibly about what was happening with Willie, she sometimes wished that she had been able to have a quick fling with him and end it neatly. She enjoyed what they did together, and she was continually surprised by the depth of the affection she had begun to feel for him. But she had also begun to have the sense, partly provoked by what Willie had done for her, that she wanted to clear out her life and perhaps start something new. The thing was that when Vicky thought about what had happened to her over the last fifteen years, she often felt a kind of surprise that she had somehow arrived here, in her late thirties, as if she had travelled without noticing how far she was going, only to fetch up at the end of a long wide plain, which, when she looked back over it, seemed to have very few notable or even recognizable features. That was her life. It hadn't seemed like that when she was married, and during that time she had even put a different sort of value on her career. Now it seemed as if she had done nothing worthwhile, not even produced a child, especially that, as she was beginning to think more and more often. And along with that thought would come the betrayer's whisper, to which she listened with burning and frustrated ears – perhaps it was not too late; and perhaps there could be more in her future than she'd been willing to allow herself. These were thoughts she played with furtively, like solitary fingers between her drowsy thighs late at night. But something had changed since Willie's friends had arrived, and Vicky was beginning to have the uneasy feeling that everything, not just matters in the house, but everything about her life was somehow beginning to spin out of control.

The only one of her three lodgers who had a clear understanding of what might be happening in Vicky's mind was Byron. One of the great things about being in the nick, he often told Sonia later on, was that it trained you in practical psychology. It had to be practical because your survival depended on understanding people and what they had in their heads because if you didn't you might mess with the wrong con, or make the wrong decision about how to deal with a dozen situations which might threaten your life every day.

Byron had prided himself on the fact that he could rely on the sharpness of his perceptions. So from the time he'd moved in he had read both Vicky's confusion, and her incoherent craving, the way he would have read a con who was nursing some aching greed deep inside him. From that moment he'd begun, even without knowing it, to kick around, in the back of his mind, a number of vague plans for using her emotions against her.

So when Willie told them that Vicky wanted them out, while Sonia reacted with a predictable outburst of paranoiac anger, Byron sat quietly reflecting and trying to follow up the clues that were floating around in his head about how to gain a few more days and keep Vicky quiet.

The next day he set out early for George's address. By about eight he was standing by the bus stop looking, as casually as he could manage, at the front of the house. He was conscious that one or two people looked at him oddly, but he took no notice. Obviously they weren't accustomed to seeing young men loitering on the pavement out there, but unless someone was going and coming pretty regularly in a short time he guessed that they would assume he was waiting for a bus.

Round about eighty thirty the woman, who Byron took to be George's wife, came out and drove away in the Mini Metro, with the schoolgirl beside her. Half an hour later George, whom Byron recognized from Sonia's description, came out and drove sedately past. He was fortyish, with a head of brown hair going a little bald, glasses, and a pepper and salt beard. He didn't look much like a bookie. But then, Byron thought, bookie shop managers probably didn't look much like bookies anyway. Nothing happened after that, and Byron guessed that the house would be empty for the rest of the day. After another half an hour he decided that the woman must have a job too, and she'd be out until three, same as the day before. He wondered how he could make sure, but short of following her in a car, he couldn't think how to do it, and, his mind preoccupied with the technicalities of his surveillance, he hopped on the bus and set out for West London.

It was on the tube just pulling out of Finsbury Park station that he had his idea about how to handle Vicky. He thought about it, trying to work out the various possibilities attached to the concept, but after it had popped into his head he couldn't get rid of it or imagine any other alternatives, and in the end, walking up Harrow Road, all he could think about it was that either it would work or it wouldn't.

'We need a car,' Byron said to Sonia, almost as soon as he got back. 'It's hopeless without one.'

'I could rent one,' Sonia said. 'It would be like just an old van though.'

What she had in mind was an ancient transit van which stood in the yard at the depot, and which Charlie and Vange used from time to time, but Charlie had loaned it to her to move her belongings, and she reckoned that she could probably persuade them to let her borrow it for a few days if she dropped them a few quid. They hadn't parted on the best of terms, but luckily she hadn't had a go at Charlie or anything, just taken her wages and left, so by now she reckoned Charlie would be feeling guilty. That was one of the funny things about her. She had to get into a rage to sack anyone, because she felt so bad about it, and now, after a couple of days, Sonia guessed that Charlie would be ready to do her a favour, as long as it didn't cost her anything and even more so if she got a drink out of it.

While Sonia went off to make her arrangements about the van, Byron looked after Juliet, and it was only about an hour and a half before he heard her key in the lock. She came in, grinning, and threw a set of car keys down on the table.

'Bingo,' she said.

An hour later they were on their way back to North London, with Byron driving and Sonia nursing the baby in the back of the van. Byron did not possess a driving licence, but he didn't think it necessary to tell Sonia this. After all, he thought, he was a good driver. It was just that he hadn't got around to getting a licence yet.

They parked up the road from George's house, round about half-past two, waiting for the woman to come back in. There didn't seem to be any signs of activity, and Byron guessed that the pattern they had seen the day before was what the family did every day. If he was right, then everything was all set, except for Vicky.

During the next few minutes he told Sonia exactly what he had in mind. She listened, spellbound, the expression on her face changing from scepticism to incredulity to amusement, then back to scepticism again.

'It won't work,' she said. 'Number one she's too tight-arsed, and number two I don't fancy it.'

Byron sighed impatiently.

'Come off it,' he said. 'She's going to notice something sooner or later, especially when Ray and Louis get here. Either we sort her out or piss off somewhere else, and I don't fancy looking for another place to stay, and I don't fancy her telling the cops that we've been acting suspicious or whatever. We've got to do one thing or the other, and if we can nobble her like that we've cracked it. If you don't want to get involved I'd just as soon pack all this in and piss off somewhere else.'

Byron meant it, but he also knew that this threat would bring Sonia round, and, after she'd thought for a moment, she nodded her head submissively.

'All right,' she said. 'But if it doesn't work it's all down to you.'

She lifted her head and glared at him angrily. Byron shrugged. For some reason the thought crossed his mind that Sonia might be jealous, but he was so accustomed to thinking of her as a young sister, that he dismissed it immediately. Even so, it was an idea that wouldn't quite go away, and he began looking at Sonia with different eyes, noting the curve of her breasts as she bent over the baby, and seeing the way her buttocks swelled out against the fabric of her jeans. The image of Maureen spread out on the floor of the van in Moss Side crossed his mind and an erection began to swell in his trousers. Just then he caught a flash of red out of the corner of his eye, and his head jerked round automatically to follow the Metro as it made the turn into the drive in front of George's house.

The events of the day before were beginning to repeat themselves. The Mini Metro parked, and the same woman got out.

'Her name's Rhona,' Sonia said, gazing at her with narrowed eyes, 'and the kid's called Mandy. Rhona and Mandy.' Her tone was sarcastic. 'I bleeding ask you.'

Once Mandy had arrived, they waited for another half hour, then drove back carefully.

That same evening Byron began putting his plan into effect. They had fish and chips and baked beans again. It was the food that they'd eaten most throughout their childhood, and strangely none of them had got fed up with it. Willie had begun to eat with the other two over the last three days, instead of with Vicky, who seemed to have spent most of the evenings out at one meeting or the other or shut in her study reading, and after the meal Byron left Sonia to clear up and knocked on Vicky's door.

'Willie told us,' he said, once he was inside. 'I just wanted to say thank you very much for letting us stop here, and sorry if we made a nuisance. We really appreciate it anyway. Thanks a lot.'

He turned to go, but before he could get out the door, she called out to him, as he knew she would.

'I didn't mind your being here. Really,' she said earnestly. 'It was just that I'm used to an empty house. Lots of space. But you know you're welcome here any time if you need a place to crash for a night or anything like that.'

Vicky could afford to be generous now she'd won the battle. In fact she had feared that Byron and Sonia would take it badly and she was intensely relieved at Byron's polite and emollient manner. So much so that she felt a rush of guilt and good feeling towards him.

'It's all right,' Byron said. 'Me and Sonia can sort things out.'

'Where will you go?' Vicky asked.

'We might go up to Brighton,' Byron said. 'Sonia knows some people there.'

Brighton was the first name off the top of his head.

'Do you need money?' Vicky asked. 'It won't be much, but enough for the train fares?'

Byron thought a bit.

'I dunno,' he said. 'I'll ask you if we do.'

'You really ought to sort out some kind of job,' Vicky said.

She now felt relaxed enough to bring her professional skills into play.

'I've been thinking about that,' Byron said. 'But you know how it is, I've been trying to get myself back together mentally. It's really hard getting back into the world.'

'I know,' Vicky said sympathetically. 'I know how hard it must be.'

Byron sat down.

'Maybe you could give me some advice,' he said.

Vicky was all attention. Byron went on to tell her that what he really wanted to do was to go to college and study to be a social worker. As he talked Vicky wondered whether he was winding her up, but from the hesitancy of his manner and the sincerity of his expression she guessed that he was serious.

'Are you sure about that?' she asked. 'I know that from the outside being a social worker might look quite attractive but I'm not sure I'd recommend it to anyone else.'

Byron went on to explain how when he was a kid growing up in homes the only person with whom he'd had a consistent relationship had been a lady social worker who had been kind to him, and when she had got married and gone to live abroad, he'd felt lost and alone. This had really happened, but what Byron didn't tell Vicky was that he hadn't liked the social worker very much, that she had a moustache and hair up the inside of her thighs which he could see when he got the occasional peek up her short skirts, and her breath smelt funny when she held him by the shoulders, stared him earnestly in the face and asked him questions like – do you think behaving in this way is a good idea?

But the story convinced Vicky, as he had suspected it would, and she began taking down books from the shelves and offering him passages to read, and telling him where he could make inquiries about going to college and getting a grant. Unexpectedly, they were getting on like a house afire, and by the end of the next hour Vicky was certain that, somehow, she had got through to Byron. When he said that they were planning a celebration the next evening to thank her she agreed with no suspicion, and a feeling of distinct pleasure. Later, on the telephone to Jill, she commented cynically that they were probably up to something, but in her heart she thought that this might just be one of those times she'd experienced before when you did something generous, without thinking about it, or even grudgingly, and the recipient turned out to your surprise to have some unexpected vein of gratitude and responsiveness about them. That night, when Vicky went to bed, she listened to the kids clomping about, and even to the sound of the baby crying, with a comforting feeling of benevolence, thinking that, as she had said to Jill, enough was enough but it hadn't been totally unpleasant to have them around.

Next day was Friday, and Byron arrived at his station near George's house in good time to see the Mini Metro leave and pull out into the traffic behind it. Rhona drove to a comprehensive about half a mile away, dropped off Mandy, then continued down the road towards Oakwood tube. At the next corner after the station she turned left, pulled in and parked. Byron drove past slowly, parked half-way up the road, and from his vantage point saw her walking across the pavement into a florist's shop. He gave it ten minutes, then when she didn't come out he made a three-point turn and drove back past the shop. Looking over, he saw Rhona behind the glass, dressed in a violet overall, squirting at the flowers with what looked like a large perfume bottle. That's it, he thought, she works in the florist's, probably part-time.

Having worked out where Rhona usually was during the day, he drove back to the house. George's car had gone, there was no movement in or around the house, and he guessed that everything was wrapped up for the day, and that this was how it usually was. He looked at his watch. It was time to get back, and begin setting up the other part of his plan.

Chapter 11

Sonia and Byron went shopping. Sonia had checked out what she wanted in a cookbook, and they went down to the nearest big supermarket and picked up chicken, chillies, oranges, grapes, extra virgin olive oil, balsamic vinegar, coriander, basil, peeled and frozen prawns, apples, breadcrumbs, soy sauce, mint, two bottles of wine, a half bottle of vodka, a tin of pineapple chunks, a jar of Paul Newman's hot pasta sauce, a tube of tomato purée and French bread sticks. Byron made Sonia put the garlic back, but she insisted it was necessary, so after a while it went in the basket. A lot of the other stuff went into the pocket Sonia had under her coat, but when they came out it had still cost them nearly twenty quid.

Back at the house, Willie had dropped in for his lunch break, and he looked at the groceries with grateful and appreciative eyes. He knew that they were trying to soften Vicky up, so that she'd give them a few extra days, but he felt it was because of him that they were going about things in such a nice way; it made him think that they really cared about his feelings, and he went back to work whistling, and rapping in a falsetto voice under his breath, the way he did when he was feeling cheerful.

'I hope,' Sonia said to Byron, in a voice of warning, 'that all this is going to be all right with Willie. You know what I mean. It's not fair really.'

'Leave off,' Byron told her. 'Willie's going to get as much out of this as what we are, and as far as I can see we're doing most of the work.'

The truth was that Byron wasn't that worried anyway

about Willie's feelings, because he had once again begun to take Willie for granted, the way he did when they called him El Segundo and Willie followed him all around, and Byron looked after him in the playground, pointing out little girls he could chat up and warning bigger kids off pinching his dinner money.

That afternoon they didn't bother going out to north London. The weekend was coming up, after which they'd still have Monday, the day before the big race, to check out that George's routine hadn't changed, so they busied themselves with the job of getting ready the celebration, as carefully as they knew how. By the time that Vicky got home the house was alive with the warmth of cooking. There was something in the oven, and all four rings on the stove were occupied with bubbling goodies.

Byron had rented a video that Vicky hadn't seen, and actually didn't want to, but when they told her that she was supposed to sit and watch it, while sipping the drinks that Byron had concocted, their expressions were so pleased, and eager to please, that she felt it would be churlish to say so. Vicky did make a point of getting things absolutely clear, however.

'I hope,' she said, 'that all this doesn't mean you think I'm going to change my mind. I'm sorry. You can stay over tomorrow but after that you'll have to go.'

She felt a bit cruel saying it, but as she told herself, it's best to get things out in the open. But it didn't seem to put a damper on the kids' spirits. Byron grinned at her, then made a face of wide-eyed innocence.

'We know that,' he said. 'I told you, we don't mind really. It's all right.'

Reassured, Vicky sat down to watch the movie, which began with several naked men in a sauna and soon erupted into a fist fight, where two men crashed through a window into a bank of snow. In spite of herself Vicky quite enjoyed the sight, and she found herself watching the men's bodies with an eye of critical appreciation. She hardly ever drank vodka either, but she realized that Byron regarded vodka and orange as the sort of refined tipple a lady like her might like, so she drank a couple of glasses dutifully, and then demanded a glass of wine. In fact all this was so strange, being treated like this in her own house, that Vicky found herself relaxing as she might have done if she'd been away for something like a weekend conference. The house seemed familiar, and yet not familiar, with strange smells emerging from the kitchen, the weird film of cars crashing and men hitting each other processing before her eyes, and Willie sitting next to her on the sofa grinning happily. Half-way through the film, when Byron was out of the room opening the bottle of wine, Willie put his arm round her and kissed her. It was a shock because he had never done such a thing. Their intimate moments had occurred almost exclusively when he came to her room at night and snuggled into her bed. But at that moment it seemed part of the good feeling which had suddenly been generated in the house, and she returned his kiss with a grateful affection. So they sat, eventually cuddling each other and only drawing away a little when Sonia or Byron came in. This was the first time she had flaunted her relationship with Willie like this in front of someone else, and Vicky felt an intense pang of daring, sweet and yet somehow painful.

The dinner was odd but, Vicky had to admit, quite tasty. Sonia had used a recipe from one of her own cookbooks, a present which she'd never opened except to skip through the pictures, and so she was surprised by the hot, salty taste. She ate as much as she could, paying lavish compliments to Sonia, who beamed and frowned with important pleasure. As the meal progressed, she found herself getting more and more giggly and silly, the way she would have been with Jill or one of her other friends, and from time to time she reflected on how odd it was that she could feel so relaxed with these kids, who only a couple of days before had been getting on her nerves so much that she wanted to strangle them. But it was the drink, of course, she realized, as she drained her glass. Byron was drinking a couple of cans of Red Stripe. Willie didn't like the taste of wine, so he had merely sipped from his glass, and had taken much more kindly to finishing the vodka and orange. Sonia had confessed to feeling lightheaded after a couple of glasses of wine, and Vicky, with a feeling of genial superiority, had polished off the bottle and started on the next one. She hardly ever drank that much, but as she reflected later, it had crept up on her, sitting at her own table in her own house, and of course, while she'd been eating the rich salty food the wine had been simply refreshing at first, like drinking draughts of cool clear water. Towards the end of the meal Sonia went off and came back with a Polaroid camera with which she took photos of them all, Vicky with her arms round Willie and Byron, Vicky making childish faces, and all the other silly poses she could remember from the time when she and friends used to take snapshots. Then they all looked at them and screamed their heads off laughing.

Vicky offered to clear up and wash the dishes, but they wouldn't let her, and she got up from the table tittering a little to herself at the sheer incongruity of their behaviour. As she did so, she stumbled and swayed a little, knocking over her chair, and she might have fallen, but Byron gripped her arms and helped her upright.

'Embarrassing,' Vicky said, screeching with laughter. 'Setting a rotten example.'

She had been thinking about going to bed, but Byron led her into the sitting-room and switched on Willie's CD. The only light on was the small lamp in the corner; in the near dark the room seemed to throb dangerously with the deep vibrations of the bass sound, and somehow Vicky could feel the notes resonating right inside her.

'Bong, bong, bong, bong,' she muttered, as Byron put his arms round her and they began to dance, Vicky stumbling a little and trying to find the rhythm.

'I'm no good at this,' she told Byron earnestly.

'Never mind,' he said.

He began showing her how to do it, holding her hips tight against his and then swaying and grinding. Vicky giggled, because the motion was like an absurd parody of sex.

'All this is obscene,' she said firmly. She was referring to the lyrics coming out of the CD, but when she said it she realized that the same could be said for the way that Byron's erect penis was nudging and rubbing against her crotch. She pulled away from him a little.

'You are a very bad boy,' she said. 'I don't think I should be doing this.'

It struck her that she was behaving in a silly way, which wasn't at all like her. But then, she thought, she didn't know quite what she was like any more. She had drunk too much, she knew, and the trouble was that drinking too much made her randy. It was an equation which had been in force since she was a teenager and she'd gone with Julian, a boy who was already in the sixth, to her first party, where they'd turned the lights out and snogged, and she'd ended up behind the couch, with his fingers rasping unpleasantly in her groin, and the sound of her best friend, Andrea, groaning and yelping in her ear. Something about what was happening tonight had taken her memory right back to the sickening excitement of that time, the dark, the dizzying sense of being almost out of control, and when Byron had pressed himself up against her she'd hadn't withdrawn, instead she had felt her belly and her thighs pushing forward steadily, her body going soft and pulsing sweetly.

She pushed him away suddenly, and shook her head.

'I need some coffee,' she said.

They made their way to the kitchen, Byron's arm round her waist, holding her up. In her confused state, Vicky had more or less forgotten about Willie and Sonia, so it was a double shock when Byron pushed open the kitchen door, and she saw Willie lying back on the kitchen table, naked from the waist down, while Sonia bent over him, like a cat nuzzling some savoury morsel, the tip of her tongue delicately lapping the tip of his penis. Vicky felt a high, wailing sound emerge from her chest, involuntarily, as if escaping her best efforts to hold it back, and Willie turned to look at her, his face as shocked as she imagined her own features were.

'Sorry,' Vicky said ludicrously, turning to go and stumbling a little, so that Byron had to catch her and hold her up again.

He slammed the kitchen door behind them.

'Stupid kids,' Byron said soothingly in Vicky's ear. 'It's the booze, y'know, and Willie always fancied Sonia. But it's just 'cause they're pissed.'

Vicky pushed away from him.

'Willie is entitled to do what he likes. Goodnight,' she said, in a voice of frozen dignity. She put her hand on the banister and began climbing the stairs. It seemed like a huge effort, but she managed it without falling over the stair carpet as she was dreading, and at the top she headed for her room, her back straight as a poker, went in, and closed the door sharply behind her.

Byron went back to kitchen, a sly grin taking over his face. This wasn't quite how he had planned the evening, but it was going well enough so far. As he pushed open the door, however, Willie was struggling with his trousers, worry and contrition lining his face.

'What's the matter with you?' Byron said satirically.

'I've got to go and talk to Vicky,' Willie replied anxiously. 'Did she say anything?'

'Yeah,' Byron said. 'I was a bit worried like, but she just smiled and said you were entitled to do what you liked. Then she said she was knackered and pissed and all and she was going to bed and get some sleep.'

'You're sure she wasn't kind of,' Willie gestured, 'fed up?'

'Nah. Course not,' Byron reassured him. 'She's a grown woman, isn't she? She knows these things happen. She said.'

Willie still had that uncertain look and Byron switched the subject.

'Here. Have a drink. Settle your nerves.'

He handed Willie the remains of the vodka.

'Drink up and let's go next door, listen to some music. You don't want to go rushing up there like a prat. She'll just think you're a stupid kid if you do.'

Willie drained his glass, then the three friends walked across into the sitting-room, Sonia and Byron with their arms entwined round Willie's shoulders, and tumbled on to the sofa.

'You're not worried that she'll chuck you out, are you?' Byron asked in a sarcastic tone, returning to the attack. 'Don't worry about that, mate. It's me and Sonia she wants out. Once we're gone everything will be hunky-dory. You wait and see.'

'What about the job?' Willie asked anxiously. Byron's remark had reawakened his guilt. He'd still be safe and snug in here, while they were out on the street, but at least he could show he was still on their side when they went to do the bookie.

'No problem,' Byron assured him. 'We'll still do it.'

Sonia held Willie's head and turned him towards her, staring into his eyes.

'Come on,' she said. 'Everything's all right.'

She lowered her voice to a private whisper.

'Don't leave me now.'

At the same time she unzipped Willie again and slipped her hand into his trousers, stroking him expertly. Willie was stiff as a board, which was no surprise because he had spent as much of his youth fantasizing about Sonia as she had about Byron, and for him, this was like a dream come true. Eagerly his mouth found hers, and she lay back on the sofa, drawing him on top of her.

'I'll go and see about Juliet,' Byron said. 'And I'll go in and have a little chat with Vicky. See she's all right.'

Willie made a strangled sound which Byron took for consent, so he got up and went quietly out of the door, shutting it tight behind him. Swiftly he mounted the stairs, a feeling of sheer glee rising irresistibly inside him. On the landing he opened the door of the room where Juliet lay sleeping and peeped dutifully in. Then he turned and went down the passage to Vicky's room. Outside her door, he tried the handle and pushed. It opened silently, as he knew it would. None of the doors in the house were ever locked, apart from the bathroom door which had a small bolt on the inside.

'Vicky,' he whispered into the dark, shutting the door behind him.

There was no answer, but as his eyes grew accustomed to the gloom, Byron could make her out, lying on the bed. She hadn't closed the curtains and in a moment he could see her clearly, flat out on her stomach, her face turned away from him and buried in the crook of her arm. She had taken off her dress because now she was only wearing a T-shirt, and he could see her shape, the pale skin of her legs and buttocks gleaming faintly in the reflected light from the window. Byron paused, transfixed by a strange idea. Looking at her, he was overcome, not so much by the desire to fuck her, although that hadn't gone away, but by the odd feeling that she was posed, just for him, like a picture in a book, and he wished at that moment that he could paint her or take a photo, one of those real artistic ones, like in the books he used to flip through in the library.

Vicky wasn't asleep, but when she heard Willie, which was who she thought it was, whispering her name the way he usually did, she didn't feel like answering. In fact she couldn't think what to say, and in any case there was something about the way she was feeling which stopped her opening her mouth. She had been lying there, one part of her busily thinking about Willie and what she had seen, but what she was thinking seemed irrelevant and somehow beside the point, trivial. For instance, she'd wondered at first about the fact that when she saw Willie's prick loosely grasped in Sonia's hand she'd experienced a little thrill of surprise at how large and angry it looked, because the funny thing was that she couldn't remember ever having had a good look at it in the light. Most of the time when he came to see her in bed it was in the dark, and afterwards he would go off to his own bed some time during the night. She liked it that way, but she'd never bothered to ask herself why. Not seriously anyway. That was the sort of idea which occupied her mind as she lay there, but the other part of her was numb, as if she'd taken some kind of paralysing drug and was now stretched out there, incapable of movement. As in a dream, there were dark bonds encircling her, so that she couldn't even waggle a finger to save her life. Under all this Vicky was feeling a kind of hurt which she was determined to deny. After all, she argued to herself, Willie was a boy, and however it had gone between them, she could be seen as the aggressor, the one who had taken advantage of his youth and naïve strength for her own enjoyment. If he wanted to play games with someone his own age, she hesitated, thinking of their colour, someone like himself, well, he was entitled.

With all this swirling round inside her, Vicky couldn't respond when she heard her name, and she simply lay there supine and passive, while he sat on the bed beside her and began to stroke her back slowly and deliberately. After all the confusion of the last half hour Vicky gave up and simply surrendered her body to the sensation, and in a few minute she began drifting off and then coming back, all the time experiencing a lethargic but increasing pleasure from the soft massage she was receiving. When the hands moved between her legs, she spread them wider to give him access and as the fingers probed gently between her wet lips, she began lifting and lowering her hips against them. Suddenly, it struck her that there was something familiar, yet strange, about the way she was being touched. Willie had never done this, and in the same instant she remembered Byron pressing his dick against her and she knew that it wasn't Willie. She turned round and sat up with a jerk, her head dazed and swimming, as much from the trance she'd been drifting into as from the drink.

'Byron?' she said.

She heard him murmur something, but she couldn't make out what it was. His hands were still on her, between her legs, stroking her thighs, and somehow she couldn't muster the strength to stop what he was doing.

'Wait a minute,' she said. 'Wait a minute. Where's Willie?'

He didn't answer and she guessed that Willie must be with Sonia.

'Wait a minute,' she said feebly, hearing how feeble she sounded.

She gripped his arm and instead of pulling it away from her, squeezed as hard as she could.

'All right,' he said suddenly. 'One minute.'

Incredibly he began counting.

'One, two, three, four, five, six . . .'

Vicky sighed, somehow unable or perhaps unwilling to think any more. She stared into the dark for a couple of seconds, listening to Byron – 'thirty-one, thirty-two, thirty-three' – then she lay back and relaxed, closing her eyes, and when Byron stopped and moved forward against her, she spread her arms and her legs for him, and as she felt his weight come down on her, she moaned a little and held him tight.

It was certainly different, she thought later on. Willie was vigorous, but he didn't waste much time getting in and coming to an orgasm, whereas Byron seemed to be dedicating himself to playing with her body, looking at her all the time through his slitted eyes, pausing and making her wait, while he touched and squeezed her trembling body, lying taut and still with his hard bulk deep inside her waiting and waiting – 'Do you like that?'

That was how it seemed to Vicky. In fact Byron was hardly thinking about Vicky, or about anything at all. Byron was in heaven. Now he was doing precisely what he had dreamed about for years with the sort of woman who might have emerged from one of his fantasies. It wasn't simply the fact that Vicky, when you got her clothes off, had a beautiful body. Maureen had possessed an even more impressive body, but the whole thing had been swift and sordid, a few minutes bumping on the floor of the van and then rolling aside to strip off the condom and dump it, while the girl got up and straightened her skirt, and the brothers cackled and hooted at the speed with which he'd dropped his load. Afterwards he could barely remember her face or how she'd responded while he was doing it.

Vicky was different. For a start she was classy. Her face had the sort of cold, calm, bossy look of someone who was always in charge, and when she'd started rubbing up against him downstairs he'd felt an excruciating thrill as he saw her face soften and her eyes waver as he looked into them, and he knew right then, he just knew that soon he'd have her like this under him, gasping and clutching and trembling when he jammed his cock hard into her. The best thing about this feeling, he thought as he rammed into her, was the way he could master a woman like this with his dick, and make her cry out and groan and ask for more. He bent his head, bit her nipple and smiled when she gave a yelp. 'Do you like this?' he asked again.

Chapter 12

The next morning went down in Vicky's memory as one of the most difficult and unpleasant times in her life. She had woken up with a sense of foreboding, although the traces of what had happened on the previous night remained as a residue of dark, almost hysterical excitement. That was partly due to the hangover, and in her first minutes of consciousness she lay still, exploring her headache, and the queasy feeling in her stomach. Then all the night's events flooded back into her mind, clear-cut images exploding in her head, the sight of Sonia and Willie on the kitchen table, the sensation of Byron's hands on her while she writhed and squirmed below him. A feathery quivering began somewhere in her stomach and rippled through her, emerging as a groan. She groaned again, this time in real agony as she thought of going downstairs to face Willie and Byron. What would she do? What would she say? She'd been foolish before, she knew. But this was unmanageable. Crazy.

In the event it was some time before she saw either Willie or Byron. She heard Sonia and Juliet going out, she presumed for a walk or something. Then she went down to the kitchen, which somone had already cleared up. That was one thing about the institutional way they had lived, she thought. Well trained. She made herself a cup of tea, took it back to bed, drank a few sips, and drifted off again.

It was well past noon before Vicky got up again. She shut herself in her study and began to read. She was half-way through a book about Daphne du Maurier, and somehow, by coincidence, it was the right choice, because it more or less began to settle her nerves as she read about Daph's unconventional affairs, and the length and breadth of her entanglements.

'Oh well,' she muttered to herself, 'I'm not doing that badly.'

In an hour or so she felt better, almost ready to face whatever the day might bring. But by the end of that afternoon she was to look back on that hour as a kind of lull before the storm, when she had managed to deceive herself that everything would really be all right the same as before.

Vicky had been turning things over in her mind while she read a few chapters. After an hour she came to a bit which said that women were like geography: 'from sixteen to twenty-two, like Africa part virgin, part explored. From twenty-three to thirty-five, like Asia – hot and mysterious.' Vicky laughed and laughed, unable to stop herself, an edge of hysteria bordering the sounds she heard coming from her mouth. She was, she supposed, now 'like the USA – high toned and technical', which was the next category, but the truth was she felt more like Africa, and if there'd been a continent which was clumsy and thoughtless and randy all at the same time, that would have been her, she thought. She shut the book with a snap, and stood up decisively. She would have to talk to Willie. That was all. But when she went back upstairs to look for Willie, he didn't seem to be there. His bed had been slept in, but she supposed he had gone out without her noticing.

In the kitchen, Byron was sitting, slumped in front of the table, swigging at a mug of coffee.

'Hello,' he said. 'The kettle's on. You want some coffee?'

The question was so mundane, after all that had happened, that Vicky had to suppress a giggle. At the same time she was glad that he had spoken first, because in the moment she saw him, she had realized that she could not think what to say to him, and she had started, unusually for her, blushing. She was red with embarrassment, the thought of it making her even redder and more embarrassed. I haven't done that in years, she thought, and she felt a spurt of anger with Byron and Willie and the whole lot of them.

She made her own coffee, without speaking to Byron, apart from giving him a nod, a brief smile and a curt hello. Byron didn't seem to mind, his only reaction being to sit up straighter, and she noticed, out of the corner of her eye, a sly smile, which for some reason she found threatening, coming and going on his face.

When the kettle boiled and she'd made her coffee, she turned to carry it back to her study, and she'd just reached the door when Byron spoke.

'Thought I'd better tell you,' he said, 'we've got a couple of friends coming Monday night. They're just going to stay one night, they'll be off on Tuesday. Then I reckon me and Sonia will get off about Thursday.'

Vicky stood stock still, gripping the handle of her coffee mug tight because as she listened to him she could feel her hands beginning to tremble, she wasn't sure whether with rage or fear or mere shock. A few seconds passed in which their eyes met. Vicky's face was red again, her gaze blazing at Byron, who met it with a cool sarky smile. At last he looked away, picked up his cup and drained it.

'I thought we'd settled all this,' Vicky said. 'You and Sonia and Juliet are going by tomorrow at the latest, and you won't be having friends to stay here in any case.'

Byron met her eyes again, and now his smile was definitely triumphant. 'That was before last night,' he said. 'We had such a good time I reckon you wouldn't want to chuck us out the way you said. I mean.'

Vicky took a deep breath. Now that the first shock was over, she knew that she had to handle this with some care, and she was thinking furiously about what to do.

'Last night was,' she gestured, 'last night. It's not going to happen again, and it does not change anything I said before. I want you to leave. Do you get that?'

'What are you going to do if we don't?' Byron asked, his tone idle, like a cat playing with a mouse, and at that moment this was how he saw himself.

Vicky thought deeply about the answer to that, but said the first thing that came into her head.

'I'll have you thrown out, you unpleasant little shit,' she said furiously. 'This is my house, and I don't give a damn about what happened last night, you can get out right now and take Sonia with you, and Willie can go too if he wants.'

Byron was a little taken aback by the force of Vicky's reply. He had expected her to be more cowed, and the thought crept into his mind that if he wasn't careful he might go too far, and that maybe Vicky was the sort of person who just might cut her nose off to spite her face. No normal person would, but he knew from bitter experience that there were people you just could not reason with once they got past a certain point of anger, and it wouldn't make sense to push Vicky till she went berserk.

'Wait a minute,' he said. 'Wait a minute. I'm not talking about stopping for ever or anything. It's just that we've got something to do on Tuesday and if we can't stop everything will fall apart, and we'll lose the opportunity. If you just let us stay here till then, we'll be gone. That's a promise. We'll have enough money to get our own place or do whatever we want to do. That's straight up. Ask Willie, if you don't trust me. He won't lie to you.'

Vicky glared at him, trying to work out what was best.

'What's this opportunity?' she said eventually.

'I can't tell you,' Byron said. 'You don't want to know anyway. Let's just say we'll be gone after that.'

'Suppose I don't let you stay,' Vicky said, and she could have bitten her tongue for saying it, because she saw Byron relax by the tiniest of fractions and she realized that he knew now that she might be about to give in.

'I don't know,' Byron said. 'That would just make problems for us, and I don't know what would happen when we all got mad. It's a lot easier just to stop a few days. We won't get in your way.'

Vicky stared at him, undecided. She had a nasty feeling that if things went as far as throwing Byron and Sonia out against their will, the trouble they could make for her would be uncontrollable, cataclysmic. In that instant, she could see the leering face of her supervisor, whose efforts to get her into bed she had resisted with a cool disdain, which she knew galled him. If her relationship with Willie, or indeed the way she had behaved on the previous night, got back to the people at her office, she really would be incapable of facing them again. There might even be legal implications to the way she had carried out her guardianship of Willie, and when she thought about that she knew that she had to compromise with Byron.

'Tuesday?' she asked him, trying to sound as firm as she could.

'Thursday at the latest,' Byron said, smiling nicely.

By now it was obvious to Vicky that he must have planned the whole affair meticulously. She should have guessed, his considerate manner the day before, the lavish meal, the 'souvenir' Polaroids that Sonia had taken while they were at dinner, the discovery of Willie and Sonia on the table. She wondered also whether Sonia might have taken more pictures of her while she was asleep, but right then she couldn't bear to ask.

'What about Willie?' she said. 'Was he in on your scheme?'

'Wasn't a scheme,' Byron said, smiling again. 'But you don't have to worry about Willie. All this will surprise him, believe me. Anyway, he thinks the sun shines out of your thingy. You know what I mean?'

That was the point at which Vicky began rethinking how she would approach the situation. Later on, when she called Willie into her study and told him what had happened, she believed that his indignation was genuine. What comforted her, and made her think that perhaps there might be something to be salvaged from the wreck of her good deeds, was the fact that he reacted with concern about her. As she had thought, Willie had been so inebriated the night before that he hadn't noticed Byron going into or coming out of her room, and when he knew everything he was full of rage and contrition. Vicky watched him steadily, knowing now that she had a weapon which she could turn against Byron.

'I want you to tell me everything,' Vicky said, looking him in the eye. 'Everything they're doing.'

Chapter 13

By the time Louis and Ray turned up on Monday night relations in the house had settled down into an uneasy and watchful state of truce. Vicky had said to Byron that while he and Sonia stayed she would be happy if they kept out of her way as much as possible. She wanted to use the kitchen, for instance, until seven after she came in and she wanted them to avoid being there at that time. As for when their friends came on Monday night, she wanted them confined to the kitchen and the sitting-room and the little loo with the basin downstairs. In no circumstances were they to climb the stairs, or enter her study. Byron assented with a serious look of agreement, but inside he was doing his nut. Not because he wanted anything different to happen, but Vicky didn't half piss him off when she laid down the law like that. Why couldn't she just pretend that nothing had happened?

But even while Byron nursed these angry thoughts about Vicky's style, he found himself eyeing her body with a barely controllable lust. He couldn't get out of his head the way she had felt and moved, and the soft nubbly tenderness of her nipple when he licked it with the tip of his tongue like a ripe and bursting raspberry, and when thoughts like this overcame him he found himself having to nip into the downstairs loo for a quick wank to calm himself down. He didn't dare to try and repeat his coup with Vicky, because he knew that things were different and now she would never let him. Even worse, he had a nasty suspicion that if he tried anything at all that Vicky thought was out of order, it might drive her over some edge of tolerance. He didn't know what might happen then, but there was something about the icy contempt of her gaze which made him uncomfortable, and he didn't want to find out what she might do if she really lost control and went for him. Willie, too, was acting strange, his manner sullen and withdrawn. Willie had never been like that and Byron couldn't understand it, but somehow he couldn't get through to the boy.

So it was with some relief that Byron set out on Monday morning to mount his surveillance at George's house. Everything happened as usual, and this time Byron followed George, driving at a distance all the way up through north London into the West End, carefully timing how long it took George to get in to work. It was about an hour and a half, but the traffic was bad coming into Camden Town that day, and Byron reckoned the normal time would be not much more than an hour. Back at the house they discussed carefully their plans for the next day, and then Byron drove Sonia over to south London to drop Juliet off with Mrs Holland.

They hadn't been back very long when the brothers arrived. The funny thing was that Sonia and Willie were somehow thrilled and happy to see Louis and Ray, even though when they remembered the triplets they thought about them as nutters and weirdos. The brothers, who normally had little interest in anyone outside their immediate circle of three, were on their best behaviour for the occasion, even though they insisted on telephoning Mohammed immediately to let him know that they had arrived.

They went out to stock up with chicken McNuggets and tins of lager, then came back and sat in a circle on the floor while Byron explained in detail what they were going to do next day. Then Louis and Ray showed Byron how the two guns they'd brought worked. Sonia would have nothing to do with it, and looked away all the while they had the weapons out in the open. Willie stared with a horrified fascination, but shook his head when Louis offered to show him. After Byron had pointed one of them, and pulled the trigger, and practised putting the magazine in, the brothers put the guns away and everyone relaxed a bit. Then they watched a Chuck Norris video, which they all declared to be well wicked, and then they went to bed, Byron and the brothers stretched out on the sitting-room floor, still surrounded by the chicken cartons and empty tins. They were all keyed up, but after a couple of pints each, sleep wasn't too far away.

When the alarm clock woke Byron he looked over at the brothers but they were already awake, sitting up weirdly like statues, muttering quietly to each other. He wondered what they were saying but then he heard what sounded like a rhyme and he realized that they were muttering poetry to each other the way they always did. The door opened, and Sonia came in fully dressed, carrying a tray full of tea cups.

'Looks like a good day for it,' she said.

Byron didn't have the slightest idea how she could tell, because it was still dark, but, unlike Sonia, it took him a while to get going in the morning, and he merely grunted at her.

In about half an hour they were driving up past Oakwood station, Sonia at the wheel, Byron and Louis in the back. On the way they rubbed Sonia's white lipstick on their eyelids and all round their eyes and mouths. Looking at Louis, Byron saw a face which had been transformed into a clown's mask and he grinned, feeling a lift in his spirits. He made a sad clown's face at Louis to give him a giggle and they pulled faces at each all the way down until Sonia stopped at the bus stop opposite George's road. Suddenly sober, the two boys got out.

'Good luck,' Sonia said. She hesitated as if she was going to say more, but Byron waved his hand, and she shut up, made a U-turn and drove away.

It was not yet six, and although they could see grey streaks on the horizon, there was no one on the street to see them walking silently down opposite pavements towards George's house. They had decided to start early for precisely this reason, so that when they got into the house there would be no pain in the ass neighbours watching or hanging about to make trouble for them, and as far as they could tell it seemed to be working. They dodged across the front garden and round the side of the house, moving swiftly like shadows in the morning gloom. Byron reached over and unlatched the gate barring the path beside the house. Beyond it they could see the back garden, and they went in, shutting the gate quietly behind them.

This was the moment at which Byron decided that it was all real, it was all happening and he was going to do it after all; and when they found the kitchen window open at the top he decided, also, that it was going to be a lucky day. They fitted on the balaclavas and the gloves, so that all that showed was their eyes, and maybe the whitened skin around them, and Louis jumped up on the window-sill, reached in through the open pane and undid the catches. Then they eased through the little window, standing on the kitchen sink, and jumped down lightly.

The house was dark and silent, reminding Byron of when he used to take out the papers for Mr Singh, and he used to get up round about this time and walk quietly through the hall shutting the door softly behind him so as not to wake anyone. In his memory it was mostly winter, his footsteps leaving a trail in the thin crust of frost all the way down the pavement.

He considered the situation. There was no point in going upstairs to wake them up. He and Louis had got into the house unheard and unobserved, and that was the main thing. They could wait quite happily until George or Rhona or Mandy came downstairs. Over the next hour they explored the lower part of the house, read George's letters, and opened every drawer and cupboard they could find. There was very little in the place that interested them, apart from a cache of five hundred quid in a desk drawer and a pile of videos with titles like *Colour Climax* and *Tammy Goes to Town*. The sitting-room was nice, though, with a big black leather sofa and armchairs to match. You could stretch out on the sofa and watch the TV, which had a kind of screen that neither of the boys had been close to before, absolutely flat, and about four times the size of a normal TV screen.

'Bloody hell,' Louis said. 'This is all right.'

He stretched out his full length on the sofa, put his gun on the floor beside him, and closed his eyes. Byron looked at the gun. It worried him a little, but he knew they needed it, and in any case there was no way that he could have persuaded Louis to leave it behind.

It wasn't until about half-past seven that they began to hear sounds upstairs. First the toilet flushed, then Byron heard steps coming down the stairs. It sounded like an adult, too light for George. He guessed it would be Rhona. She came to the bottom of the stairs and went past the half-open door of the sitting-room without looking around, dragging her slippered feet a little and yawning. Byron caught a glimpse of her as she went by. It was a sort of shock to see her so close up when he'd watched her so often from a distance, like an animal, a lion or something, that you'd seen on the telly hundreds of times, and then found yourself facing it, just on the other side of a flimsy fence at the zoo, or the wildlife park where they'd been one time in their foster-mother's car, baboons suddenly glaring at them just on the other side of the glass, making Sonia scream out loud.

Rhona was in her thirties, her profile a bit younger than he'd thought when he saw her driving up in the Metro. It was a pretty face but sort of ordinary, like any number of women he might see in the street. She was wearing a short cotton nightdress, her dark hair curling round her neck in a disordered mass, and as she went he could see her bum. It wasn't bad too, a bit heavy, low down. Her legs seemed quite short, with big sturdy thighs, but her skin was firm and smooth, a light tan outlining the thin strip down the middle where her bikini must have been, and Byron thought that even though she wasn't in the class of Vicky, she looked great, getting a hell of a kick out of watching her half naked and unaware that he was standing there while she walked into the kitchen.

After she'd disappeared he eased the gun that the brothers had given him out of his belt, drew the magazine out of the handle, put it in his pocket, and, feeling better about it, walked quietly behind her to the door of the kitchen. Rhona was filling the kettle. Byron sensed that she heard him coming, but she must have assumed it was George because she didn't look round as she put the top back on the kettle and clicked the switch on. Byron had considered how to handle it. He didn't want her to go hysterical, which she might if he touched her, so while her back was turned he lifted the gun and pointed it straight at her head, so that it would be the first thing that she saw when she turned round.

'Rhona,' Byron said. 'Turn round very slowly, and don't make a noise.'

Byron wasn't sure what reaction he'd get but what Rhona did next was the last thing he'd been expecting. Instead of fainting, or leaping in the air, or screaming, Rhona put her hands behind her, lifted her nightdress, bent over a little, wiggled her bum at him, then turned round, a mocking smile on her face.

Byron was shocked and startled at first but immediately realized that Rhona must have thought it was George, playing games, because when she saw the figure behind her looming in the dull light, its face covered by the balaclava, the gun pointing only a couple of feet away from her face, her mouth dropped open, her features settling into a rigid mask of shock and horror. A weird sound, half-way between a groan and a shriek, emerged from her throat, and Byron held up his other hand.

'Shush,' he said quickly, 'shush. I won't hurt you. I'm not going to hurt anyone as long as you keep quiet. Keep quiet and you won't be hurt.'

He stood there making shushing sounds – sssh, sssh, sssh, until Rhona seemed to get what he was saying, a kind of sense returning to her eyes, and her mouth closing. In the circumstances she recovered quickly, Byron thought, and he made a mental note to be careful about her.

'What do you want?' Rhona said, her voice quavering. 'There's some money downstairs. You can have it. Five hundred quid. You can have it.'

'We've got it already,' Byron said. 'Just finish making your tea. Go on.'

'Can I put something on?' Rhona said.

'No,' Byron told her a little impatiently. 'I'm not bothered. Just make the tea.'

The kettle was boiling, and Rhona went about the tea-making, moving slowly at first as if in a dream, then a little more briskly, sneaking apprehensive glances at Byron as she did so. He waited till she'd finished, then motioned her to walk ahead of him into the sitting-room. She got to the door, then stopped as she saw another masked, armed figure standing in the corner, but Byron shoved her gently from behind and she went in.

'Call the rest of them,' Byron told her quietly. 'Call

them down and tell them to come in here, and don't do anything stupid.'

'Can I put my coat on?' Rhona asked. She pointed. 'It's just there on the banister.'

Byron stepped out into the hall and got it for her, feeling that a hurdle had been crossed. She'd asked him for a favour and he'd granted it to her. She even said, 'Thank you,' as she took it and put it on. Then she went to the door and called out, her voice surprisingly firm.

'George. Mandy. It's nearly eight. Get up. George.'

In a minute they head the sounds of the bathroom in operation, but no one appeared down the stairs.

'What are they doing?' Byron whispered. He had been putting on what he thought of as a funny voice, and using his strongest cockney accent, which he hoped would leave them fooled. All of them had decided to try to keep George and his family in the dark about their colour, so that they couldn't be definite about any sort of description, and although Byron couldn't be certain that there was any difference between his voice and a white man's, he was trying his best to sound like one of the white Londoners who might be a customer at George's shop.

'They're washing first,' Rhona whispered back.

Louis hadn't spoken. They had agreed that he would say nothing or only what was absolutely necessary, and Rhona had begun to cast her eyes over at him from time to time in the same fearful way that she'd looked at Byron at first. In fact his presence seemed to have changed their relationship, because she was now behaving as if Louis was a threat from which Byron was her protection, and when she turned to Byron her look was almost ingratiating.

It might have been a matter of minutes but it seemed a very long time before they heard a heavy footstep on the stairs. Louis was standing in the corner of the room by the bow windows, out of sight of the door. Byron concealed himself behind the open door, and when George clattered into the passage Rhona called to him as he went past towards the kitchen.

'George. I want you.'

George came in quickly. He seemed in high good humour, rushing up to Rhona and seizing her in a bear hug.

'Hello hello hello,' he said, clowning. 'Where you been then? Been out in the garden communing with nature, have you?'

Just then he caught out of the corner of his eye a glimpse of Louis by the window, and did a quick double-take. At the same time Byron pushed the door half closed, and pointed the gun at George's head.

'Morning, George,' Byron said. 'Just keep quiet and sit down.'

'What's going on?'

George didn't sound cowed or frightened. His eyes narrowed and he glared at Byron defiantly.

'Just sit down,' Byron said, as reasonably as the voice he was putting on would let him. 'Just sit down, and no one will get hurt. We'll tell you what's going on in a minute, but right now just sit down and keep quiet and no one is going to do anything rash or dangerous or get their bollocks shot off or anything else like that. All right?'

George looked down at Rhona.

'Did they touch you?' he said.

Rhona shook her head, and, after a reluctant second, George put his arm round her. Then they went to sit on the sofa, Rhona cuddling up to her husband as if she took him for a tower of strength.

They waited in silence for Mandy, who, when she arrived downstairs, was already in her school uniform, her brown hair neatly brushed. Mandy took in the situation at a glance, and apart from goggling a little, and asking her parents several times what was going on, didn't give any trouble about going to sit quietly next to them on the sofa.

When they were all arranged like this, in a line, Byron addressed them, speaking carefully in his disguised voice.

'I'll tell you what we're going to do,' he said. 'George is going in to work, same as usual. He's got a little job to do for us, and you two are going to have the day off at home with us till he gets back. You're going to ring up the school and your work and tell them you're sick. If everything goes all right, nobody will get hurt, there won't be any trouble and when George gets back everything will be hunky-dory. If you want to make trouble it won't be like that. See this gun?' He showed it to them. 'It shoots. Right? You want to see it shoot?'

No one answered. They were all staring at him, frozen, not a muscle moving, as if paralysed by the sight. Byron shifted the gun to his left hand and pulled the big carving knife out of his belt where he'd stuck it when he picked it up in the kitchen.

'Take a look at this knife,' he said. Suddenly he stabbed out with it, jamming it up to the hilt into the leather skin of the sofa, then ripped it out, cutting a gash from which padding spilled.

'It cuts. Very nasty. I'm just showing you this to let you know we're not messing about, so don't fuck with us, because you won't like what happens. Do you understand?'

Again none of them answered, until Byron repeated the question, then George nodded his head. Byron looked at Rhona.

'You understand? You'll be all right. We won't touch you or hurt you or anything as long as you do exactly what you're told, and George. But if anything goes wrong, you're in the shit.'

He stared at Rhona until she nodded.

'All right,' Byron said in a reassuring tone. 'We're in business.'

He beckoned George off the sofa. George stood up reluctantly and when Byron turned to lead the way outside he stood stock still.

'I just want to talk with you,' Byron said. 'Don't worry. My mate will look after them. Come on.'

George didn't look exactly reassured, but he followed Byron out into the hallway. Byron climbed half-way up the stairs then made him sit on the second stair with his back turned.

'Try and be reasonable,' Byron said, 'or this could turn nasty. What we want you to do is go into work same as usual, take in all the money and that same as usual, then bring it home with you, give it to us and we'll shove off, just like that. No trouble for anybody. It's not your money, but it's your family. Right?'

'It's not worth it, mate,' George said, 'there's never that much money in the shop.'

'You're disappointing me, George,' Byron said. 'I don't know what money there usually is in the shop, but I know that today is the Gold Cup and your shop is bound to take well over thirty grand, so don't try messing with my mind. I know you'll have a lot in.'

'I'm supposed to bank it,' George said.

'Jesus,' Byron said, 'this is getting ridiculous. You know as well as I do that they can't check on whether you banked it or not until the next day anyway, and usually you just stick it in the safe and leave it. So don't keep on fucking with me.'

He said this last bit angrily, fuelled by the realization that he might have said too much, and right then and there he felt like giving George a good slap over the head with the gun for trying to be such a cunning bastard.

‘Tell me the truth now,’ Byron said. ‘I know what happened, so don’t lie. Did you bank last night?’

George hesitated.

‘No,’ he said eventually.

‘That’s right,’ Byron said. ‘You’ve got to keep some money in the shop for today. Haven’t you?’

‘Yes.’

‘I told you,’ Byron said, ‘don’t try to be a cunning bastard or else things could turn nasty. We’ll be following you all the way into work. We know exactly how long it takes so if you even stop on the way we’ll know. There’ll be someone among the customers in the shop watching you all day with a mobile phone. If the cops show up, or you disappear for longer than it takes to do a quick pee, we’ll be gone, but if you put us to all that trouble your family will know about it.’

George bowed his head a little so that Byron saw the back of his neck. There was a spot, he noted with distaste, right in the middle.

‘All right,’ George said. ‘All right.’

‘Just one thing.’ Byron lowered his voice. ‘I’m reasonable. That’s why I’m the one talking to you, but some of my mates are nutters like him in there. For God’s sake don’t do anything to get them nervous or upset them. Bad enough as it is, I can tell you. I’ll be honest with you, I’m happy nicking your firm’s money, but I don’t really want to do anything to you or your wife and daughter. But it’s up to you. You mess us about and the situation will get seriously dodgy, mate.’

‘All right,’ George said again. ‘All right. I’ve got it.’

Chapter 14

The drive into work that morning was like a horrible parody of George's normal routine. He was more or less on automatic pilot, and at the same time he was trying to calculate what his options were. If he found some way of quietly getting in touch with the cops, or with the firm's security men, or even getting a message to the area manager, he might be exposing his daughter to a horrible fate. Images of Mandy and Rhona lying dead or subjected to some kind of horribly obscene attacks flashed through his head. Yet even if he did what they said, would they keep their word? In the end he decided that it was more likely than not they would simply accept the money and leave his family alone. They had nothing to gain by going over the top, he reckoned. Even so, a nagging terror of what might happen kept on poking through the surface of his decision, and by the time he reached the shop he was sweating with anxiety.

He had been examining the road behind him carefully to see whether he could see a vehicle following him, but whoever they were, the bastards were impossible to spot, and although when he wheeled his car into the small car-park near the shop he checked the cars going past, he couldn't work out whether he had noticed any of them before. His only hope now, he thought, was the coolness of the guy who had spoken to him, and he hoped that he was sufficiently in charge to keep everything under control, and moving smoothly. It was the sort of thing you learnt in the Territorials, which George had been a member of over the last ten years. If the leadership was confident and competent not much could go wrong.

Once he'd opened the shop he moved into his usual routine. He'd been open late the night before, covering the greyhounds at Monmore and Bristol, and the evening horses at Chester. All he'd had time for was a quick go with Terry, and afterwards they'd gone down the pub for a drink before he set out for north London. It was funny how these things happened, just when everything was going smoothly. He hadn't got home until nearly eleven, and Rhona had been a bit moody, so he'd chatted with her a bit and they'd gone to bed as soon as he'd finished his supper. In the morning George had come awake, still buoyed up by a feeling of pride that he'd been able to perform so effectively with Rhona, even though he'd given Terry one only a couple of hours before.

'Life in the old hot dog yet,' he'd said to Rhona, thinking that she had no idea how much.

But as usual he now found himself with a load of little jobs, which he would normally have taken care of after he'd closed up, and he began settling yesterday's bets swiftly, his mind racing through the simple computations and covering the slips with bold red ink.

Siobhan and Geraldine came in half an hour later. Terry and Liz were on late so they weren't due till lunchtime, but by about ten when the first two came in, there were already customers beginning to queue up, eager to collect their winnings from the day before. Some of them were equally eager to hand over their money on the day's meetings, and as the morning wore on the shop began to acquire the excited hum that went with the everyday business of gambling.

George opened the safe to get out some money for the tills, and gloomily considered its contents. Better than seven grand in there, and he speculated on his chances of concealing it from the others. If they were going to do the shop anyway, it would make sense for him to knock off a piece for himself. The fact was that all this would completely ruin any chance that he might have had of making manager of the month in a hurry, and with old Moishe retiring soon, he wouldn't have much chance of living this down soon enough to compete for area manager. Bugger it, he thought, might as well be hung for a sheep, and while Siobhan and Geraldine went round the shop putting out fresh betting slips, he casually transferred about two-thirds of the money in the safe to the pockets of his coat, which he carefully folded and stuffed into the big drawer of the desk at which he sat in the back of the shop. Now he was committed and he'd have to go along with the robbers, and play his hand out. After all, he thought, echoing the masked gunman's threat, it's not my bleeding dosh, but I've only got one wife and daughter.

By coincidence Rhona was thinking about George at much the same time, and hoping he was all right and would make whatever the right decisions were. The man who had first burst in on her, and who she now thought of as the nicer one, or, to put it another way, the one who wasn't so terrifying, had made her telephone the flower shop and then Mandy's school to say that they were ill and weren't coming in that day. She thought she'd carried it off OK, but still wasn't sure that Tony had believed her. That this was a bit of a problem only struck her when she had to talk to him. Admittedly he was a very tasty bloke, but she also had to admit that, flattering as it was, his attitude was getting to be a bit much lately. It wasn't something that she'd foreseen. She'd started work at the flower shop the year before, when they closed down the primary school at which she'd been the secretary. From the beginning Tony had given her those special looks. He was half Italian, he had told her, and he had the big soft brown eyes to prove it. He also had the wandering hands, but the truth was she quite fancied him. He was younger than her, for a start, not yet thirty, tall, with a good body and a flat stomach. A bit different from George. Not that her reaction to Tony was anything to do with how she felt about George. She still loved George, even though they'd been together more than twenty years. They'd been childhood sweethearts at the same comprehensive Mandy now attended, and when they left school and George started on the counter in the local bookie's, her dad was flabbergasted. Her dad drove a train, one of the real working class when it came to the bleeding work, he'd say, and he was shocked about George choosing to spend his life taking advantage of working people's weaknesses. Rhona had been working in the building society then, could have been a manager herself by now if she'd kept on, and her parents thought George's job was a bit of a comedown. But he wasn't anything like one of the chancy wallies who hung round the bookies. If anything he looked more like a bank clerk, a bit round-shouldered, wore glasses, and in the last ten years he'd been developing a bit of a paunch. Not that it put her off, their sex life was still perfectly all right, especially after she'd invested in some of the old Janet Regers and a few assorted mail-order naughties. Men were so predictable really, as she often said to her mate Tina.

So she'd known exactly what Tony wanted, even though he was nearly ten years younger, but to be fair, she'd resisted anything more than a kiss and a cuddle in the office, although she couldn't resist going a bit weak when he touched her up, as he did every time they were alone and unobserved. But a few months ago, on Tony's birthday, when, as it happened, Madge, the other woman in the shop, was on her day off, he had insisted on taking her out to lunch. An expensive lunch too, at the bistro round the corner frequented by the top executives from the Mall and from firms from miles around. They'd had too much champagne. It had also been raining heavily that day. Some people said rain was a turn-off, but it had the opposite effect on Rhona, like a heavy snowfall, a curtain between herself and everyday reality, behind which she could spin off into any kind of fantasy; and when Tony said he was going to leave the shop closed for a few minutes while they had a quick whisky in the back, she agreed readily, feeling that sense of delighted and wicked luxuriousness she only ever used to get on holiday abroad, sitting out by the pool at sunset, sipping a foreign cocktail and eyeing up the talent for the night. But that had been years and years ago, before she married George, when she used to go on holiday alone with Teens. On the loose, old Teens would say, waggling her eyebrows. The holiday feeling should have told her what was coming next, and in a way it did, but she went down the back with Tone anyway, and not too long after she was sitting on top of him on the old squeaky sofa in there, deliciously straddling his long, thin penis, which seemed to have sprung into her hand the moment that she relaxed in his arms and touched the front of his trousers. The next day, laughing, he confessed that it hadn't been his birthday at all.

Typical, Rhona said to herself, but a few months later, to her surprise, Tony was still going strong. Because he was married too, she had assumed that it would be an occasional fling which would become ordinary and fade as time went on, and in her case, this was what happened. Most of the time, she thought, her mind was so taken up with fetching Mandy after school, and whether to get lamb chops or chicken for supper, that a quick bonk on the sofa during her lunch hour, which was all the time she had for shopping, was coming to be at best an irrelevance, and half the time a bit of a nuisance.

So she knew that what she was hearing in Tony's voice

on the phone was disappointment, the randy little sod. I'm going to pack it in anyway, she told herself. This time she meant it, because there was already something about a man pointing a gun at her and holding her hostage which somehow told her that her life could change in any direction she wanted.

After the phone calls the man had taken her back into the sitting-room where Mandy was sitting, her hands tied in front of her. Rhona protested as vigorously as she dared, but they wouldn't untie Mandy and instead began tying her own hands as well. Rhona asked if she could change. And the man followed her upstairs and watched her while she dressed, clumsily trying to keep her body concealed under the long overcoat. While she did this she wondered, in spite of herself, whether it would help if she could turn him on, and another part of her shrank with terror at the thought that he might at that moment be planning to jump on her. But he did nothing of the sort, merely watching her intently while she climbed into jeans and a sweater, then waving her down the stairs ahead of him.

By this time it was round about eleven, and Byron felt as if he'd already done a full day's work. He looked at his watch, hoping that everything was going according to plan, that George was being sensible, that Sonia and the boys were on the ball. He signalled to Louis and they went out into the passage together, shutting the sitting-room door behind them, so as not to be heard. It was about the time they had arranged for Sonia to pick Byron up.

'I'm all right,' Louis replied when Byron asked. Byron could sense him grinning behind the mask. 'This is a doddle. Don't worry about a thing.'

After Louis had gone back in Byron fitted the hood of his anorak over the balaclava, drawing it round his face, and put on his dark glasses. It might look a bit funny, he thought, out in the street, but no one would challenge him, and if anyone saw him leaving, they wouldn't be able to describe the person they'd seen. As he slipped along the side of the house and over the front garden into the road, he saw no one, and he didn't encounter anyone face to face on the way to the corner. Sonia was waiting in the van, just out of sight, and Byron piled in quickly, relieved that it had been so easy.

'How's it going?' he asked Sonia immediately.

'The boys are there right now,' she said. She lifted the mobile phone. 'Ray just rang in, and he reckons everything is quiet.'

At the time Ray had been standing in a phone box, near Shaftesbury Avenue, on the fringes of Chinatown, just round the corner from George's betting shop. He was dressed in a version of the messenger gear that Willie wore every day, tracksuit, a woolly hat covering his head, goggles and a cyclist's breathing mask. Nobody looked twice at a boy dressed like that in the streets of central London, and the group had decided that it was the perfect way to mingle with the crowd of customers in the bookies and keep an eye on George at the same time. In theory, as Louis had pointed out the night before, there was no way they could tell whether George was passing secret messages to anyone, but if he deviated in any way from Byron's instructions they could ring Louis immediately to get out of the house and pack in the whole caper. Their second line of defence would be to have Sonia patrol George's neighbourhood to make sure that the cops weren't sneaking up on Louis unawares. Byron had been a little dubious whether they could spot a surprise attack, but the brothers had assured him that it would be impossible for any kind of police operation to be mounted so secretly and swiftly that they wouldn't have at least half an hour's notice.

Willie had begun watching George as soon as the shop

opened, popping in and dawdling over the papers. He guessed that the manager would have his eyes open for strangers, but this was a well-frequented shop, in an area where people came and went continually, and at any one time there were up to a dozen people in the shop. They had planned spells of an hour each, and by the time Byron and Sonia reached the area it was almost Byron's turn to take over from Ray.

He drifted into the shop, resisting the temptation to seek out George with his eyes, but after he'd looked around a bit he knew exactly where the manager was, and he knew he could keep an eye on him without being noticed. It was a big room, the size of a small hall with padded seats running down the middle, and lined with monitors for the closed circuit TV. The betting windows were up one end. Behind them four women were sitting and behind them George was at his desk, settling the bets, and talking occasionally on the telephone. That worried Byron but obviously it was part of the business, and they couldn't stop him. What reassured him, however, was the fact that there were at least a couple of dozen men in the shop most of the time. There were three or four women too, but the impression you got looking around was predominantly male. Some of them didn't seem to be betting either, or at least they didn't go up to the windows during the time Byron was there, so it was obvious no one would notice a bike boy hanging around for an hour. This was one of the shops frequented by Chinese, and there was a big group of Chinese men standing in one corner. After a while Byron realized that they came and went continually, and he imagined that most of them came in during a break from their work in one of the Chinese restaurants or supermarkets, which lined the nearby streets. Beneath his mask he smiled when he saw them walking up to the counter and paying in fifty pound notes, imagining the same notes lining his own pockets.

At exactly one o'clock he saw George pick up the phone, and as he listened, the expression on his face changed. This would be the phone call from the house in north London which they had arranged at that time to remind George about his wife and daughter.

Back at the house Rhona felt a flood of relief at hearing George's voice. She knew he was in no danger, in comparison with her and Mandy anyway, but it gave her a reminder of normality to hear him, steady as ever, as if there was nothing out of the ordinary happening. Behind him she could hear the blower calling out the prices, and he imagined for a moment the busy shop with George behind his desk, calm and in control of everything.

'We're all right,' she told him. 'Don't worry. We're all right.'

She had to put the phone down then, because the big man with the gun waved it impatiently, and when she tried to say something else to George, he took the receiver firmly out of her hand and slammed it down. She looked at him indignantly, the thought flashing through her mind that even if this was a kidnapping and robbery he could at least try to be pleasant about it. Just then the doorbell rang. Rhona froze. She wasn't expecting anyone, and she couldn't imagine who it would be. It rang again impatiently. She looked at the man but he shook his head. Mandy shifted as if she was going to get up, but the mask turned menacingly towards her, and she sat back on the sofa. The bell rang again, and now the sound seemed to go through the room like a whip, lashing at an exposed nerve. Then they heard the voice calling through the letterbox.

'Rhona. Rhona. You all right? Rhona?'

'It's my boss at work,' Rhona whispered immediately

towards the masked face. 'He can see my car. He knows I'm here. What shall I do?'

Louis wondered what to do. If she didn't answer the door, this wally might make some kind of trouble. He thought wildly and quickly. As usual when he was on his own he felt cut off and in a crisis, somehow disturbed, in comparison to when he had the brothers near him, but even so the solution came quickly into his mind.

'OK,' he whispered. He had been impressed by Byron's vocal disguise, and he had determined that if he had to speak he would use a Spanish voice. Louis's idea of a Spanish voice, as it happened, was the Seagull in the *Watership Down* video, which the brothers loved, and often watched. 'Open door. Speak weeth heem. But no close no door. Me want to hear everytheeng. Capeesh?'

If Rhona noticed that the last word was Italian she gave no sign. In any case she had no idea what Louis's accent was, so she nodded to indicate her understanding.

'Wait wan meeneete,' Louis said, getting dreadfully confused. 'We hide.' Some childhood memory bubbled up in his head. 'You count feeftee. Then you go door. Eef you tell, he dead, you dead, she dead.'

He shook the gun menacingly, and Rhona nodded dumbly. Pushing Mandy ahead of him, he left the room, and they climbed the stairs swiftly. On the landing the first door he came to was the bathroom. He closed it and opened the second door, which was a big cupboard. He was about to close that too when he had an idea, and pushed Mandy into it.

'You be good girl?' he whispered. 'Not make noise?'

Mandy nodded vigorously, her eyes wide, her lips clamped tight shut.

'OK,' Louis whispered. The Spanish word for girl emerged from the recesses of his memory, and he threw it in for effect. 'OK, muchacha. You wait. I come back.' He closed the door. There was a key in the lock, and he turned it, then sat back on the landing, around the angle made by the stairs.

By this time Rhona had opened the door for Tony. He was clutching a small bouquet of roses and violets, which he handed to her as soon as the door opened. Rhona looked at them, confused. It might have been some use, she thought bitterly, if the silly bastard had brought one of them Rambo guns.

'What's the matter?' Tony said. 'I thought I would drop by lunchtime, see if you're all right.'

His eyes darted past her along the empty hallway, and he lowered his voice.

'George isn't in, is he? I checked to see if the car was there. What's wrong? Have you seen the quack? Can I come in?'

Rhona hadn't thought what she would say, and she didn't think she looked ill enough to pretend, so she said the first thing that came into her head.

'It's Mandy,' she said. 'She's got mumps.' That should put him off, she thought.

'Oh, I've had it,' he said immediately. 'I'll just come in for a bit.'

Rhona knew full well what kind of bit he meant, but somehow she didn't have the strength to invent anything else or work out a way of keeping him on the doorstep. Besides, it would look funny if she just stood there chatting to him. It wasn't what you did in this neighbourhood.

As she hovered, Tony took his opportunity and pushed past her into the hallway. She shut the door behind him quickly, and rushed to catch him up as she strolled into the sitting-room, casual as if he owned the place.

'You'll have to go in a minute,' Rhona said. 'George will be back any minute now. He's getting the afternoon off, because of Mandy.'

She felt quite proud of that story, which she had just thought up on the spur of the moment.

'All right,' Tony said. 'I've only got a minute. I've got to get back to the shop anyway. I just came to say hello.' He leered at her. 'You know what I mean.'

Rhona rolled her eyes and clicked her tongue in irritation.

'Leave off,' she said. 'Mandy's upstairs.'

'All right. Keep your hair on,' Tony muttered. 'Just a quick cuddle.'

Rhona let him kiss her and fondle her breasts and bottom the way he liked to, because she couldn't face the prospect of standing there arguing with him, but she knew immediately that it was a mistake as Tony's breathing grew faster and his hands began wandering more intimately between her legs.

'Stop it,' she whispered urgently. 'Stop it. Mandy could come down those stairs any minute.'

'All right,' Tony said. 'All right.'

But he didn't stop it. Instead he pushed her gently against the wall behind the door.

'We'll hear her if she comes down,' he muttered. 'Just give me a minute.'

While he said this he unzipped himself. Tony never wore underpants, and in an instant the thing that she had christened his peperoni in more comfortable circumstances was thrusting impatiently against her. Now it had gone this far, Rhona thought, there was only one way to get rid of him. She calculated quickly. If they were very quiet, it would be impossible for anyone listening to guess what was happening, and if Mandy had any suspicions she could lie. Anyway, what she was doing might be saving their lives. She made up her mind.

'Shsh, shsh, shsh,' she whispered, 'don't make a sound.'

She fitted her mouth to his, gripped his dick, and began stroking it gently, while he unbuttoned the top of her jeans and pushed his hand down into her crotch. Give Tony credit, it was over in a few minutes. What she hadn't expected was her response. She had imagined herself doing it with indifference, getting it over with as quickly as possible, the way she did sometimes in the back of the shop, half her mind full of trivial problems like whether to go round to her mum's that night or leave it till the weekend. But as soon as they'd started, she found herself nearly as carried away as she had been the first time, melting round Tony's fingers, and pressing herself against him, and near the end she nearly came out with the sort of shattering groan about which she'd warned him. After that she clung to him almost a minute before she was able to collect herself, pull away, and go over to the sideboard to fetch some tissues, with which she wiped her fingers and the front of her jeans. In the meantime Tony had tidied himself up and he went immediately, as good as gold, making a soulful face at her and grinning happily as he went out through the hallway. Rhona shook her head. Men were so predictable, she said to herself, as she closed the door behind him.

Chapter 15

By the end of the afternoon George estimated that he had taken close on forty grand at least. The Gold Cup had been won by an outsider. It was one of those days when everybody was piling it on the favourites, and the outsiders were coming in. George didn't have to pay out as much as he might have done on a normal day and the money kept coming in to pile up in the safe. There were only a couple of other meetings on that day as well, and the dogs had run early. Everything had been pushed forward to make way for the big race, so all the action was over by about half past five and by that time George was already preparing to close up. The phone rang while the girls were clearing up and he was locking the door after the last customer. George almost ran the length of the shop to answer it, getting a curious look from Terry, who raised her eyebrows and made a face at Geraldine.

'You've got less than an hour to get home with that money,' the voice on the other end said. 'Don't let us down, George.'

George put the phone down, heaved a deep breath, and began clearing the tills with the girls and totalling the receipts. That didn't take long, and he told them that they could go right away. Terry said she would hang about and help him finish settling, but George told her that his daughter wasn't well, and he had to get home. She gave him another funny look and went, her stilettos rapping angrily on the floor as she left, her stiff back signalling irritation at the rejection implied by his insistence on rushing home instead of taking the opportunity to spend a little time with her.

George took no notice. He knew what he had to do, but even so he felt as if he was taking a step over a barrier between himself and chaos. He couldn't be blamed for following the kidnappers' instructions. Not when they were holding his wife and daughter. But in spite of that, he knew there'd be questions asked and, even though his mind was full of terror for Rhona and Mandy, he felt a ghastly flutter in his stomach at the thought of the investigation that would follow, and the suspicion he would have to resist once the firm realized that they had dropped an entire day's profits, plus what he'd had in the safe overnight.

He packed the sports bag that the kidnapper had given him quickly, parcelling the money with a sureness born of long habit, and stuffing it in. The bag bulged. It was funny how much space forty grand took up. He switched off the screens, picked up the bag, and took a last look around, patting the coat pocket which held what he thought of as his rightful share. An idea struck him. He could keep a lot more for himself, and he determined to dump half the contents of the bag in the car on the way home. He took the money out of his pockets and zipped it in. The last thing he wanted was notes falling out from below his coat. All his tasks finished, he looked round again, hefted the weight of the bag in his hand and went out.

He walked rapidly to the little car-park he used, not taking any notice of the bike messenger leaning against the fence as he went in. It had started drizzling a little and he hurried to put the key in the lock, but as he did so he heard a voice behind him which he recognized immediately. It was the voice from this morning.

'George,' it said. 'Don't bother to turn round, just put the bag on the ground. Get in the car and go home.'

George stared into the glass in the window. He could see an indistinct shape in the glass behind him.

'What about my family?' he asked. 'You're not getting this till I know they're safe.'

'Put your hands on top of the car and wait a minute,' the voice said.

George did as he was told. By now the rain was beginning to slant down harder and the water was trickling down into his sleeves, but he didn't move. Something touched his ear and he jerked away a little, then realized that it was a phone. It was ringing, and after the second it stopped.

'Rhona,' he said, and in a second Rhona's voice answered.

'George. Is that you, George? Are you all right?'

'I'm fine,' George told her. 'I'm on my way home. How about you?'

'Fine,' she said. 'Just worried about you.'

'No trouble? They haven't hurt you or Mandy?'

'No. No,' she assured him hurriedly. 'We're perfectly fine. Just come home.'

Her voice wailed a little at the end, and the phone went dead.

'All right, George,' the man behind him said. 'Don't do anything stupid. We don't want to hurt you. We don't want to hurt your family. Just do what I told you. We'll follow you up to the station and then we'll ring our bloke and tell him to clear off. If you try to stop and use the phone or mess about at all, it's on your head, mate. I won't be responsible. It's nearly over. Let's just get it done. Go on.'

George put the bag down, turned the key in the lock and got into the car. As he slammed the door, he had an impression of someone picking the bag up, and he turned just in time to see what looked like a bike boy threading his way through the line of parked cars and vans, but in the gathering dusk and through the rain now washing down the rear window he couldn't get a good look. He opened the side window and poked his head out to see better, but by the time he'd done that, the figure had disappeared.

In fact, Byron had dodged behind the nearest van, waiting for George to move, and in a few seconds he saw the Volvo plunge past, pause at the gate and speed away. Byron ran out and round the corner to where Sonia was waiting, with Willie and Ray sitting in the back. He tossed the bag on to the floor of the van between them, grabbed the mobile phone, and dialled the house in north London. The ringing stopped but no one spoke on the other end. That would be Louis, as they had arranged.

'We're in business,' Byron said in his assumed voice. 'Get out of it.'

'OK. Bueno,' Louis said oddly, and Byron cut him off.

They were home in about half an hour. Willie and Ray had wanted to open the bag and look inside but Byron insisted that they should leave it till they got back. He made them stick it under the seat, and cover it with some of the old junk in the back of the van.

'Suppose we get stopped,' he said. 'We don't take no chances. Right?'

The others agreed, and they rode back to west London, Sonia driving as cautiously as she ever had done.

In the house, they went to Sonia's room and closed the door. Byron came last, carrying the sports bag. On the way, he stopped off in the downstairs loo, dying for a pee, he said. But by the time he emerged, he had extracted a bundle of the notes. He chose fifties, his fingers flying, two great handfuls, and on his way upstairs stuffed them carefully in instalments under the carpet on half a dozen of the steps. On the landing he threw open Sonia's door with a huge gesture, slammed it behind him, unzipped the bag, raised it over his head and upended it to shower the money all over the bed. At the sight of all those notes flying through the air and scattering all over the room, the friends leapt up ecstatically, whooping and screeching, clutching the money in their hands and rubbing it over their faces like some kind of sweet-smelling soap. After a while they calmed down into ripples of hysterical giggling, when Byron held up his hand for silence and put his finger to his lips in a comical gesture, and after a few minutes they sat down again and began to count, piling the notes beside them on the floor in their different denominations. Willie went downstairs, and cautiously entering Vicky's study, found a box of rubber bands which they used to strap up the money. They piled the fifties in bundles of twenty, a thousand pounds each. The twenties, tens and fives they collected into bundles of fifty, and by the time they'd finished they reckoned that they had thirty-one thousand two hundred and twenty-six pounds on the bed.

Louis came in half-way through the process. He had tied up Rhona and Mandy, taken off his balaclava in the hallway and slipped out the back, his anorak hiding his face. The bus had arrived almost immediately, and the tube journey back had been uneventful. When he saw the piles of money on the bed he punched both fists in front of him and waggled his hips, and then they all shook hands, slapping their palms together with a noise like a paper bag bursting. Then they calmed down again, and settled down to finish the counting. When they'd finished it was gone nine o'clock, but no one wanted to stop and think about food or anything boring like that. They'd all been too wired to eat during the day, but what with the tension, the euphoria, and the relief of having got away with it, they were all a bit light-headed. Food was the last thing on the group's mind, and even if someone had slapped a pizza or a dish full of burgers in front of them with all the trimmings, chips, pickles and everything, it would have been more or less impossible for any of them to have summoned up the appetite to eat a single mouthful.

They'd heard Vicky come in, and after Willie had listened at the door to see what she was doing, they concluded that she must guess they were shut up in Sonia's room, and she wouldn't bother to disturb them, they thought. Not yet, anyway. So when there was no sign or sound of her coming up the stairs, they got on with it and divided up the money, a half for the triplets, and a half for the others. Byron thought about the stash he had concealed with a definite feeling of complacency, and he handed over the triplets' share with a sense of virtue, because, after all, they had mentioned fifteen grand, and they were getting more than they probably bargained for.

'We couldn't have done it without you,' he said, and the brothers, showing an unusual sign of emotion, stuck their hands out to grip both of his. After this they all hugged each other for one last time, and clattered down the stairs, with the brothers' share of the dosh safely stowed in their washbags and thrust into their case underneath the two pairs of jeans, underpants, and shirts. Then they all drove to Euston. The brothers had missed their train, and would have to get on the midnight one, but that was no problem because now everything was settled everyone suddenly felt ravenously hungry, so they all crowded round the phone booth and rang Mohammed to let him know about the train time, then went up the road to one of the Indian restaurants near Warren Street station and ordered lagers, followed by the most expensive items on the menu. By the time they'd finished it was nearly time for the train, so they all went back to the station, and hugged each other for one more last time.

'The curfew tolls the knell of parting day,' Louis said suddenly as he let Byron go, and half-way through the sentence Ray started saying the same thing, so that what came out was a sort of chorus, the two voices contrasting and harmonizing, but with the emphases all the same, both of them pausing and slowing down and raising their voices at exactly the same thing. To the other three, it was as if they'd suddenly started singing. 'The lowing herd,' they continued, 'winds slowly o'er the lea, the ploughman homeward plods his weary way, and leaves the world to darkness and to me.'

When they said 'me', both of them banged their chests at the same time and laughed. Watching them, Byron felt a rush of affection, and a weird kind of regret at the thought that he was now going to be separated from them.

'Bloody hell,' he said. 'Shut the fuck up.'

The brothers laughed again, gave the thumbs-up sign, and then they walked off on to the platform exactly in step, swung themselves up through the door half-way down the train, and stuck their heads out, grinning and waving and pretending to sick up the food they'd just eaten, while Sonia and Willie and Byron capered around and made rude gestures till the train started moving and Ray and Louis gradually disappeared out of sight.

Chapter 16

When George got home he untied Rhona and Mandy's hands. They were sitting on the sofa waiting, stock still, as if they'd been zapped into paralysis. But as soon as George untied them they came alive and clutched at him, clinging on and crying noisily.

'He didn't hurt you?' he asked Rhona anxiously.

She shook her head, and he turned to Mandy asking the same question. Mandy considered it for a moment.

'No,' she said, in a quavering voice. 'But it was horrible. I was so scared.'

After this, George got on the telephone and rang the area manager, Moishe, who reacted with a slightly disappointing lack of excitement. But, of course, Moishe hadn't been area manager for fifteen years without having experienced situations like this, or worse. He told George that he would contact the firm's security and to ring the police right away. George rang the police, and then sat down with Rhona and Mandy to wait, drinking tea. In the back of his mind he had expected half a dozen police cars to speed up to the door, with their sirens screeching, but it was more than an hour before anything happened. In the meantime Rhona rang her mum and a couple of other relatives and her mate Tina to let them know what had happened in case they saw it on the news. That was another thing. This was obviously news, and Rhona went off to do her hair and put on a decent dress, and her sling-back high heels, before any reporters or TV cameras turned up.

When the police arrived, thought, it was only two

detectives, one of them looking scarcely older than a teenager. Something George had read once about how you were getting old when the cops looked like kids crossed his mind. The detectives were accompanied by a policewoman, who ignored him and went straight over to Rhona to introduce herself.

For the rest of the night the detectives grilled them separately, making all of them go through their story at length, and asking them again and again about the details. They allowed Rhona to stay in the room while they were questioning Mandy, but she had to sit a couple of feet away and keep quiet. In the middle of all this, a van-load of other policeman turned up and began to search the house and the garden, for forensic evidence, they said, which Rhona supposed meant clues. At more or less the same time a man from the firm's security came through the door. He was a short sandy-haired man with a Geordie accent, who said his name was Hamilton, and he talked with George and the police, then said he would come back in the morning to finish up his report.

It was well past midnight before the house was cleared. George went round locking everything and checking all the windows. Fat lot of good that does now, thought Rhona as she went round in her turn clearing up the mess that the police had left. After she'd washed up, and straightened the furniture, and dusted where they'd left bits of power and sweaty handprints, and muck they'd brought in on their shoes, she vacuumed the entire house from top to bottom, ignoring George's mild protests. She went over the carpet behind the door in the sitting-room two or three times, scanning it carefully to see whether there was anything suspicious there. She had told about Tony turning up to see if she was all right during the middle of the day, but not, of course, what she'd had to do to get rid of him. She knew Tony wouldn't give her away and she knew, because she'd checked, that Mandy hadn't heard anything. But in spite of knowing that she couldn't be found out, she felt a twinge of guilt every time she went near that part of the sitting-room. Of course, if there had been anything to see, she thought, someone would already have spotted it long ago, but even so she couldn't help herself.

Eventually they went to bed. But although it was now the early hours of the morning, George couldn't sleep. Both the police and Hamilton had speculated about whether it was an inside job. They didn't seem to be suspicious of him. Mandy had done the business there, because she had told her story with so much feeling and graphic detail that it was clear the episode had happened just as Rhona and George described it. During the evening, also, the police had turned up a couple of neighbours who had glimpsed Byron and Louis leaving at different times, although all they could describe was a couple of hooded figures. George knew that he would still be under suspicion because that was how the security men were, but given time he would be in the clear. The question that wouldn't leave George's mind was who the inside operator had been, because once he'd thought about it, he was quite certain that there must have been someone on the inside. All the girls knew about his family, and so did everyone else in the firm who knew him. It wouldn't be hard to discover his address either, and the robbers had known so much about his methods and routine that it was hard to believe they didn't have some kind of inside knowledge. But he couldn't imagine one of the girls arranging this lot. Terry lived with her parents in Wood Green, and in any case he didn't believe that she could have behaved normally all day without giving something away if she had been involved. The other women were all married and respectable. He had met their husbands. One of them was himself a policeman. Never, George thought. It wouldn't be any of the girls, and as for the other managers and assistants that he knew in the firm, he couldn't believe either that any of them would take the risk. There were easier, less risky ways of looting a shop, if that's what you wanted to do.

His mind returned to the girls, and he thought, no, not one of them, and running along in that vein he suddenly came up with the image of Sonia's face when she discovered him with Terry. If she was still there, he thought, maybe it would have been her. Then it struck him that she wouldn't have needed to be working there, she knew all the necessary details already. Automatically he made a mental note to mention Sonia to Hamilton in the morning, then thought better of it. If it was Sonia, he had a chance of getting the money back. But it wouldn't do him any good if the robbers were tracked down and captured, whoever they were. It was doubtful, even, that the money would be recovered. The firm can afford it, he said to himself. The ideal thing would be to get the money back without anyone knowing, because as far as the firm was concerned the dosh was gone, and with this thought in his head George drifted off to sleep at last.

Rhona woke up when the alarm went as usual, but this time she lay there fighting against the urge to close her eyes and go back to sleep. Apart from anything else she had the sense that something great and terrible had happened which would change her life for ever. She didn't know how, but it was a bit like being ill, a feeling which overwhelmed you and wouldn't let go, and about which there was absolutely nothing you could do. It had changed her already because when she went down the stairs, nearly half an hour later than usual, she didn't wander down with her eyes half closed in the normal way. Instead she tiptoed, stopping to peer ahead of her and round all the corners, and it took her several minutes to make sure that the house hadn't been entered during the night. Going into the kitchen, she thought that she would probably never feel safe again in this house the way she used to, and she wondered idly about the chances of persuading George to make a move.

Soon after this Hamilton arrived, by which time both she and George were dressed and ready. They had intended to let Mandy lie in, but Hamilton wanted to talk to her, so she had to come down in her dressing-gown, yawning and stretching, to tell her story all over again. She was taking it well, Rhona said to George, but as Hamilton commented, the kids usually did in these cases.

George rode into work with Hamilton, talking over the ideas he'd had the night before. He didn't mention Sonia specifically, even when Hamilton said he'd be checking previous employees for the last year or so. Both of them understood it was a needle in a haystack job, because a lot of the staff were more or less transient, students, single mothers, Irish kids passing through on the way to somewhere else. George knew he was in for a morning of questions, and so were the girls in the shop, so he told Hamilton about what he'd been doing with Terry. Hamilton narrowed his eyes a bit, but eventually to George's relief he grinned, as if he knew the score.

George got home early that night, because he'd asked for the rest of the week off to take the family away and recuperate. Moishe, who normally would have agreed without argument, had to pass his request upstairs this time, but eventually he rang back to say that the district manager had every sympathy with George and hoped that his family hadn't been too badly affected. Not fucking much, thought George. He guessed that they wouldn't pursue the idea that he was involved, unless Hamilton could actually find some evidence. But he also knew that in all the previous cases like this, the manager who had been so unlucky was never trusted again, and would certainly not be granted any kind of promotion. The odds were, he suspected, that they would transfer him within a couple of months to one of the little shops in a suburb. Maybe he could move nearer home. That might be a bright spot, but apart from that, he knew that his career with the firm was effectively halted. If he could rescue that dosh, he thought, it would make up for it.

Driving home, he began thinking idly about how he could invest it. Discreetly, of course, nothing flash, steady shares, premium bonds, stuff like that, then after a couple of years when things had settled down, he could try another firm, or even go into a different line of business. He was still young enough, and by then the recession would be over and there'd be openings for the kind of small business he'd dreamed about but imagined was still a good ten years further off in his future.

Back home Rhona was moody and impatient. She and Mandy had been in for a day of interrogation, describing the men all over again, and looking at police photographs, a useless proceeding because they had no idea what the men looked like. Mandy insisted that the man had been Spanish but Rhona wasn't so sure. Greek or Turkish she thought perhaps. Their story was on the news that morning, and again throughout the day in the lunchtime local reports and later on at six o'clock. The cameras had been, and Rhona and Mandy had a sentence each describing their experience while the newsreader, one of them girls with an expensive hair-do and a funny-looking mouth, spieled about the housewife who'd been taken hostage. Rhona hated that description and it spoiled the pleasure of appearing on TV, although she perked up when the phone kept ringing and all the neighbours, together with, it seemed, everyone she ever knew, rang in to say that they'd seen her and didn't her hair look lovely. Tony had rung too. The police had come to see him, and he kept repeating that he couldn't believe it till she cut him short and slammed the phone down.

It was getting dark when George went out again. He told Rhona that he was going down the Lodge, and when he got outside he looked around carefully, making it appear as casual as he could, in case the firm had stationed anyone to keep an eye on him. He couldn't see any obvious candidates, but he took no chances, driving first to the pub opposite the station, then leaving it through a different exit, before he got back in the car and drove towards central London by a circuitous route which he rarely used. By the time he got up to Marylebone he was sure that no one was following him and he was beginning to feel a bit ridiculous about the precautions he'd taken, so he pointed the car straight into the traffic in Park Lane and headed for south London over Chelsea Bridge.

The plan in George's mind was to confront Sonia, sort of innocently, as if he had simply come to see how she was. If she was involved with the robbery, he thought, she would give something away. He was confident of that. But it hadn't occurred to him that she might have changed her address so quickly, and when he got to the house where he used to drop her off after work, and saw the boarded-up door, his heart sank. Even so, he crossed the pavement and banged on the boards at the doors and windows. He did get a response eventually, but it was from the next house down. By then he had given up knocking and was loitering on the pavement staring up at the blank windows. Suddenly a door near him opened. A tall teenager with a spotty face and a pony-tail was standing there leering out at him.

'They've gone, mate,' the teenager said. 'Been evicted.'

He gave a short sneering bark of laughter, George nodded his thanks and turned away. Then he got back in the car and sat there trying to work out how he could find Sonia. He had no idea where she might have gone. As far as he knew she had no relatives apart from the baby. But the thought of the baby sparked something, and in a short while he remembered dropping her off to fetch little Juliet at a house not far away. He even remembered the childminder's name. Mrs Holland.

George found the house without too much difficulty. When he knocked it was opened by a dumpy pale-faced woman with greasy dark hair tied up into a point with a rubber band. Her small dark eyes stared at him suspiciously as if she was trying to assess how much money he was after. George asked her if she knew where Sonia was, and she shook her head, the suspicion on her face deepening.

'The thing is,' George said, 'I've got some money for her. She left our firm about a month ago, and the money's just come through. Our letters came back, you see. So they sent me to call round, 'cause you look after the little girl. Don't you?'

'The little girl's here now,' Mrs Holland said. 'She'll come and pick her up in a minute if you want to wait outside.'

George considered. After he'd left Sonia's former address it had struck him that it would be far better to find out where Sonia lived and watch her for a while to see whether she had any associates who might be the kidnappers, before he actually confronted her.

'I don't know,' he said. 'I'm just going off. Have you got her address?'

'No,' Mrs Holland replied shortly. 'But I'll tell her to call round your firm.'

She shut the door.

George hurried back to the car. He started it and drove quickly round the nearest corner. If he stayed there, parked in front of the house, she was sure to recognize the Volvo, and he had conceived the plan of following Sonia as soon as Mrs Holland had said she was coming to pick up Juliet. He parked in the first space he found, got out and walked back to the corner. Unlike his own patch of north London, no one here would remark on a man loitering on the pavement for a while. They were all too busy minding their own business, George thought, and he stood by the side of a post-box, pretending to read the evening paper, as if he was waiting for a friend or something like that. From time to time he sneaked a glance round the corner to see whether Sonia had arrived, but in fact when she did turn up he wasn't looking. Instead he had been reading a small news item about the looting of his own shop which quoted Rhona and Mandy, as they all did. It was horrible, they quoted Mandy saying, and he imagined her saying it, the word sounding more and more dramatic and drawn out every time it emerged from her mouth. Occupied in this way he had failed to see Sonia arrive, and when he looked round again, he realized that the young woman getting into the transit van double-parked in front of Mrs Holland's house was his target. George ran back down the street to the car, fumbled the engine on as quickly as he could, and zipped out round the corner to see that the van had gone. He sped past Mrs Holland's house and at the next corner it struck him that his luck was in for the first time since the previous morning. She wasn't up ahead, but when he looked left automatically, his eye travelling down the line of traffic, he saw, only about fifty yards away, the top of a van identical to the one he'd seen Sonia climbing into.

Chapter 17

Funny how you can be up shit creek without a paddle one day and then on the very next day everything's coming up roses. As George sat parked on the next block up from Vicky's house, he reflected that this must be his lucky day, in comparison with the day before, which had been just the opposite.

It had been easy tracking Sonia back to the house in west London, poodling along behind the rackety old van. She had stopped, pulled over and walked across the road, while George continued until he found a parking space at a safe distance. Then he had noted the house. It was freshly painted, with a white front door and a fence round the front garden, all of which made it look somehow too posh for Sonia, who up till then had been living in some crap squat in south London. So George hung on and waited to see what would happen, whether she was merely visiting for a short while or whether she stayed long enough for him to conclude that this was where she lived. He figured that she wouldn't be just visiting, because that would mean keeping the kid out much later than about eight or so. But, he reflected, you never knew with these girls, so he waited. That was the lucky bit, because he hadn't waited more than a quarter of an hour before a tall black boy dressed in lycra shorts and an anorak came out and walked up the road, passing him on the opposite side of the street. Practically as soon as George saw him he ducked down behind the wheel, because he recognized the outfit at once. This was one of the customers who'd been in the shop the day before, and now he realized that he also remembered the glimpse that he'd had of the bike boy who'd picked up the sports bag in the car park. As the memory gained in clarity, he realized, also, that the impression he'd had was of someone who looked very much like this boy, not black, really more sort of brown. It was all too much of a coincidence, and his heart leapt and thumped with the understanding that he must have found the gang. Still he waited, but all that happened was that the tall boy came back in another fifteen minutes or so, walking carelessly, swinging his arms and shoulders, and carrying four white plastic bags, which George recognized immediately. Chinese takeaway, he guessed, or maybe Indian. Not that it mattered. If the bastards were having their dinner, then one or all of them must be permanently resident in the house.

George made up his mind quickly. He drove out of Harrow Road, and then turned left along it, stopping at the next phone booth that he saw. By coincidence it was situated right outside a police station, but George didn't feel the slightest temptation to go in. Instead he rang his dad in Kent. His dad had moved out there more than ten years ago, even before he'd taken early retirement. He'd been employed for most of his life in the Direct Works department at the town hall, but throughout George's childhood George had been accustomed to hearing his father complain about the fact that there was no real scope for a craftsman like himself in the job. After a while it was one of his dad's grumbles which simply went in one ear and out the other. But to George's surprise, after his mum died, his dad, who, as he said repeatedly, wasn't yet sixty, started going to evening classes to do furniture making and upholstery, and then George had to get accustomed to Rhona whingeing about the numerous pieces of badly made and lumpy furniture that her father-in-law kept on foisting on them. George had assured her that it was a phase that would soon pass, but to his surprise, not only did the old boy get better at the furniture, but he took up with one of the instructors, a woman in her mid-forties who specialized herself in arts and crafts like furniture-making and pottery. She was actually a bit posh in comparison to his mum, with a house in Kentish Town which, when they visited for dinner, seemed to be littered with arty things, pieces of pottery, old earthenware and china, antique furniture and intricately embroidered rugs and covers. George couldn't get over his dad taking up with a woman like that, or, to put it another way, as Rhona said, what does somebody like that see in your dad? But, in fact, when George thought about it, his dad had always been that way inclined, with a bookshelf at home piled high with books about art and antiques and things like Greek architecture. On the other hand, there was still something strange about the old fella latching on to a woman who had to be a pretty good catch for anybody his age, and who lived as if she could not only support herself but must have a bit tucked away in the bank too.

By the time George's dad announced that they were buying a house in Kent with a big garden and a small orchard attached, George had stopped being surprised by anything he did. But for all of them visiting his dad and stepmother had become a genuine pleasure which they could look forward to without any reservations.

'Hello, Steph,' George said breezily when his stepmother answered the phone. 'Is my dad in?'

'Of course, George,' Stephanie said in that posh way she had. His own mum had always called him Georgie Porgie. 'Here he is.'

'You all right?' his dad said immediately. 'I saw what happened on telly, and I rang Rhona, but she said you were out.'

George told him briefly that things were very hectic

and asked whether they could come down that same night.

'The reporters, the police, the neighbours,' he said. 'It's all a bit much, Dad.'

His dad agreed without fuss and George said they would be driving down later on that night. As he put the phone down he reflected how peculiar it was that his dad seemed so much happier and more fulfilled now that his mum was dead and he was leading what amounted to a completely new life. Perhaps he ought to mind, he thought, but he didn't really, because he liked his dad much more now than he used to, and in the last ten years he'd started looking up to him and listening to his views in a way that he'd never been able to when Mum was alive.

He rang Rhona next and told her what he'd arranged to do. He half expected a bit of an argument, but the fact was that Rhona wasn't unhappy to get away for a bit, even if it meant packing up at an hour's notice to leave. She was nervous in the house, she had to admit, and on top of that she wanted to take a few days off from work anyway. Somehow what had happened in the sitting-room with Tony was like a purge, clearing her mind of indecision about him. She knew now that she didn't want to keep on doing what they'd been doing in the back of the shop, because even though she'd experienced one of her most intense orgasms up against the wall with Tony she knew now that she didn't want him to touch her that way again. So she wanted to get away for a bit, not to think about her decision, but to put some distance between herself and Tony and work out how to tell him.

Perhaps she wouldn't go back at all. She didn't have to, even if it meant letting him down at short notice. She could ring him tomorrow morning from Kent. Mandy would be delighted too, she knew, because they all looked forward to seeing George's stepmother, as well as the old boy, of course. At first they had found her a bit weird with her artistic hobbies and her posh way of talking. But now Rhona was proud of her in-laws, partly because, eccentric as they were, they were definitely a cut above. In addition their house was surrounded by green fields and fruit trees, and they kept a sort of menagerie of animals, chickens, a goat, and two donkeys they had adopted from a sanctuary which had closed down. The man donkey had been a bit of a problem, because the first time Mandy pointed out the huge swinging extension below his belly and asked George what it was, he'd nearly had a fit. But Stephanie, cool as ever, had laughed and explained in detail, making it sound all sort of scientific and biological, which is more than George or Rhona could have done, and afterwards Rhona could never resist taking a long and fascinated look at the donkey's long and muscular dick, which she figured he took a malicious pleasure in displaying whenever she was around. So for the first time in two days she smiled a bit, feeling the depression lift as she imagined waking up in the morning to the sound of birds and the bright glow of spring sunshine across the fields.

By the time George arrived he had made his own plans, and they piled into the Volvo after he'd rung Moishe. He had to do this, because he didn't want the firm to think he was making any sudden moves, and he explained carefully where he would be, and how long he would be away, and how to get in touch with him. On the way down the atmosphere in the car was more or less cheerful. Mandy had been a bit hyper at first, going on about the chickens and the donkey, but then she settled down and, as they were going through the Medway bypass, drifted into sleep. At that point George told Rhona that he would be going back to London that night. In answer to her stare of astonishment, he explained that one of his mates, Andy, in the Territorials, a man whom she vaguely remembered, was also a retired policeman. Andy, he elaborated, might know something about the villains who'd held up his shop, and since he reckoned that the firm's security man Hamilton couldn't find his bottom with both hands in the dark, he wanted to see Andy and do a little checking of his own. Rhona accepted his story, merely asking why it couldn't wait until the morning, but George said the sooner the better, and he'd already made the arrangement.

He felt a bit bad lying to Rhona like this, but he figured that the less she knew the better for her, and he was only looking after their mutual interests, after all.

In a fairly quick time, less than a couple of hours, they were bumping through the narrow lane to his dad's house. They were still up. They were unpredictable like that. Most people were in bed by the time telly got a bit boring, but Steph hardly watched telly at all, and instead the couple would be occupied with making something or, oddly, reading to each other. Tonight they had been working on an old chaise-longue that Stephanie said she'd picked up in Canterbury for a few quid. They had it stripped down to the frame, which they were polishing. When George and Rhona arrived, leading Mandy, all bleary-eyed and stumbling, his dad threw open the door and hugged them all, in that extrovert fashion he'd begun to develop lately.

George explained about going back, while Rhona put Mandy to bed, and his dad didn't ask any questions.

'You'll stop for a cup of tea?' Stephanie asked.

What with the cup of tea and talking over the robbery, it was nearly gone midnight by the time he actually left, and he roared out of the lane, pushing the car as fast as he dared back along the motorway. He didn't get into the centre of London until nearly two, but that didn't worry him, because he knew that in the normal run of things Mr Chan would still be round and about. In fact

Gerrard Street was still busy, tourists still walking about and the Chinese who usually thronged the street still lounging in front of the shops and restaurants. He turned left and parked down the end of the road, then walked round the corner and went into Mr Chan's little restaurant, which he always thought of as more of a caff really. By this hour it had shut for business and as he went in someone shouted, 'Closed, closed.' Up the back there was a group of Chinese men, all seated round a big table, playing cards. Some of them seemed to be eating at the same time, and George wondered whether they cooked meals specially for themselves afterwards, or whether they were eating up what was left of the day's cooking.

'Mr Chan,' he said hurriedly. 'Mr Chan here?'

One of the men at the table got up and looked at him. George recognized him. He was one of the waiters, and he often came in to George's shop.

'Mr Chan?'

'That's right,' George said. 'I've come to see Mr Chan.'

'You wait,' the waiter said.

George waited. He wasn't worried about whether or not Mr Chan would see him, because he knew Mr Chan had said he could come at any time. They'd known each other for more than ten years, ever since George had arrived to take over as manager of the local bookie shop. Chan hadn't owned a restaurant then. He was one of the waiters, or something, in a big Chinese restaurant nearby. He'd recently come from Hong Kong, as he told George when they got to know each other better, but he wasn't one of those who'd got out with their money while the going was good. He had come, in fact, by circuitous routes, and was now committed to a period of service in which he would have to pay off the debt he had incurred, and the debt was growing larger, because he intended bringing his wife and child to join him. But George didn't know all this till later. At the beginning he'd got to know Chan because he used to come in early and bet small sums, coming back late to pick up his winnings, so that as George got accustomed to seeing him, they began to share the odd joke, Chan being something of a joker, with a different bit of word play every couple of days which he'd picked up from the newspaper or one of the customers. George never found his jokes very funny. There's definitely a cultural difference, as he remarked to Rhona, discussing the customers at his new job. But he laughed anyway, and within a couple of months Chan's was one of the faces he recognized and looked for in the district.

One morning, to his astonishment, Chan came in and asked to speak privately. Chan told him that he knew of two horses running that afternoon which would win. The problem, he said, ignoring George's polite scepticism, was that he had no money, or not enough anyway to take advantage of the opportunity. If George could give him credit, he said, he would be for ever in his debt. George tried to dissuade him. Everyone who came into the shop, he told Chan, thought he knew of a horse or several horses which would win that afternoon. It was a mug's game, he concluded, and the proof was that there were bookie shops open all over the country. Chan listened smiling and nodding courteously, then asked George whether he could do him the favour, and he added that he would go to another shop to put the bet on, if George wanted it that way. George never knew what made him do it. Perhaps it was something to do with the streak of wildness Rhona said he was indulging when he went off with the Terrs, but eventually he told Chan that he'd let him have a hundred. Chan grinned wildly, his entire bearing acquiring an almost comic jauntiness, and he immediately put the hundred on a double, two five-to-ones, which came in that afternoon and paid him a total of three thousand two hundred and forty pounds after tax.

George never knew how the waiter had known. He guessed that Chan must have overheard something at one of the tables, and in any case he didn't want to know. He'd laid a few quid himself, although he wasn't supposed to, and it had been a nice little tickle. But after this they had become firm friends, and he watched Chan's progress with growing respect. When Chan had acquired his restaurant George went there regularly for lunch, and recommended it to everyone he knew. During the times they spent together subsequently he'd got to know, through a series of vague hints, and through reading between the lines of Chan's stories, that Chan's progress had not been without its rough passages, and he understood that Chan had learned how to handle himself within the deadly competition of the area's business community. So Chan had been the first person who had come into his mind when he thought about what he needed.

The restaurant owner appeared, hurrying a little, as if to apologize for not being ready and waiting when George appeared unexpectedly at two in the morning. They shook hands, asked after each other's health, and then George cut through the small talk.

'You know what happened at my shop?' he asked.

Chan nodded, his eyes suddenly humourless and watchful.

'I need a gun,' George said, lowering his voice.

Chan didn't show any surprise, but his expression questioned George.

'They threatened my family,' George said, taking a tack which he knew would get through to Chan.

'When do you want this thing?'

'Now,' George said tersely.

'I can do it,' Chan replied. 'But impossible right now.'

George's heart sank. He had been counting on Chan and he had no idea where to turn next.

'Impossible right now,' Chan continued, smiling broadly at George's downcast expression. 'But in one hour. You come back in one hour.'

Chapter 18

Vicky had spent practically the whole of the previous day and night wondering what to do. Willie had told her what they were up to, but he'd refused to tell her the details. It wasn't that he didn't trust her, or anything like that, but he just couldn't, he said. Vicky hadn't pressured him. She knew enough, and when she tried to persuade him not to join in he said he would think about it, then avoided her for the next couple of days. On Tuesday night she knew that it had happened, whatever it was, when she saw them acting mysteriously, locking themselves away all evening in Sonia's room. What she feared was that they would be caught, and caught soon, and caught in her house, and that Willie would go down with all the rest of them, a possibility which gave her a pang of terror, like a hand squeezing her heart, and she knew that this was the reason she hadn't gone to the police and the reason why she couldn't even contemplate such an idea.

On Wednesday she had seen the item about the hostages and the looting of the bookie's in the West End, and although there was no reason to she made the connection immediately. She hadn't said anything to Willie but she was more and more inclined simply to confront them and to find out. At the worst she could stop them doing anything even more stupid, and perhaps make things easier. In another part of her mind she was angry, full of resentment and distaste for what they had done, and more than once she found herself stopping in the middle of what she was doing, staring into space, exploring the idea that she ought to teach them a lesson. It was intolerable, she thought, the way they treated everything around them, like predators, preying on people's good intentions. In Willie's case, she knew that it was partly because he didn't know any better, and partly because that was the way he'd always been treated himself. But the same thought kept recurring. It was intolerable.

By Thursday she was a bundle of nerves, only mildly reassured by the prospect that Sonia and Byron had promised to go that day, and she came home early in the afternoon in order to supervise their departure. She parked the car opposite, her mind still obsessively turning over the question of whether she should do anything and what it would be if she did, and she saw, without noticing very much about him, a man who was standing on the pavement looking around curiously as if trying to find a specific house number. She went straight up the steps and took out her key, thinking about what she would say to Byron, when she heard the footsteps behind her. She turned her head and, seeing the man who had been on the pavement, she raised her eyebrows in inquiry.

'Can I help you?'

In answer he looked down, guiding her gaze towards his hand. For a moment she couldn't understand, or perhaps couldn't believe what she was seeing, then she realized that he was holding a gun between them, only an inch away from her stomach, almost touching her.

'Open the door and go in,' the man said.

Vicky stood there numbly for a second, the key dangling from her fingers, and an angry expression crossed the man's face.

'Do it,' he snarled, making her jump.

Vicky opened the door, and immediately the man pushed her through it, crowding into the hallway behind her.

‘What do you want?’ Vicky said, recovering a little, but only a little, because she imagined now that this man must be a rapist or serial murderer, and she began trying to recollect all the instructions she’d ever heard about how a woman should behave in these circumstances. Not that he was a very clever rapist or serial murderer, she thought irrelevantly, because she could hear Sonia and Byron and Willie and the baby bashing about in the kitchen, and she wondered what the man would do when he realized that she wasn’t a solitary woman, coming into an empty house.

‘There’s several people in the house,’ she said steadily, looking him straight in the eye, making the effort to show no fear or uncertainty. ‘You’d better go, and we won’t say any more about this.’

As soon as the phrase had come out of her mouth she felt an insane impulse to giggle at its ridiculousness. For a moment the man seemed to be appreciating the humour because he smiled, but the next thing he said disabused her of that idea.

‘That’s right,’ the gunman said. ‘Where are they?’

‘Who do you mean?’ Vicky asked him.

She wondered whether this could be a policeman from some kind of special unit. Then she dismissed the idea. There’d be more of them in that case.

‘The bike boys,’ the man said, ‘and Sonia.’

Vicky couldn’t conceal her surprise. Now she was confused. Perhaps this had something to do with Sonia, and from the sound of it he also knew Willie. Perhaps it was something in their past which she hadn’t heard about.

‘What room are they in?’ the man asked.

Vicky listened.

‘The kitchen, I think.’

‘Let’s go,’ the man said.

Byron and Sonia were at that moment discussing the

issue of where they were going. Byron wanted a holiday, while Sonia wanted to find a flat into which she could move with Juliet immediately. Now that she had better than five grand to dispose of there was nothing to stop her. Byron was suggesting that they should all go off to the seaside, or somewhere like that, for a few days and have a rest, when the door opened and Vicky came in. It took a few seconds before they noticed the man with her, but they all recognized him immediately, and there was a stunned silence in the room, broken only when Juliet, sitting in the corner with her building blocks, burst into a loud wail.

'I can see you know who I am,' George said. 'I know exactly who you lot are. Hello, Sonia,' he continued.

He gave Vicky a little shove in the direction of the table.

'Why don't you sit down?'

He waved the gun and they all sat down round the table, so that they were all looking up at George, like a class of attentive kids. No one said anything, largely because all four of them were more or less in a state of shock.

'Right then,' George said toughly. Standing there with the gun in front of them all, dominating the situation, he felt tough. 'Where's my money?'

'What money, mate?' Byron said innocently. 'I dunno what's the matter with you, but we don't look like we're in the money. Do we?'

In different circumstances he could have been convincing, George thought, but even though his voice was a lot different to the way he had heard it before, George knew that it was the same person.

'Your voice has changed,' George told him, 'but I know it's you. I'm not here to mess about. I know it was you lot. You're still dressed in the same clothes even.'

He pointed at Willie, across whose face flitted a definite spasm of guilt and surprise.

'Listen to me,' George said. 'If I get the money back, all of it, you might stay out of the nick this time. If you mess me about you're up to your necks in the shit.'

'I don't know what you're talking about,' Byron said.

George addressed himself to Sonia. 'You could be inside for five years,' he said; he was plucking that figure out of the air since he had no idea what sentence they could get. 'What would happen to your baby then?'

Sonia, who had been glaring at him sullenly, didn't answer but her eyes flicked sideways at Byron. George had spotted a telephone perched on the sideboard, and now he went towards it, still pointing the gun at them. He picked up the receiver, and began dialling 999.

'Wait a minute,' Vicky said. 'Wait a minute. What have they done?'

George put the phone down.

'Who are you?' he asked. 'Their mum?'

He was being sarcastic, because she didn't look in the least like their mother, even though she was older, and when he had accosted her and forced his way inside, her manner had not been that of somone who knew what was going on, unlike the phony innocence that he was getting from the boy sitting opposite.

Vicky stared at him coldly. Now there were other people present she had recovered her confidence, and somehow, George didn't frighten her.

'I'm their social worker,' she declared. This wasn't strictly true, of course, but Vicky guessed that George wouldn't know exactly what a social worker did and what the limits of her authority would be. 'I'm responsible for them. You can talk to me about whatever it is they've done.'

George laughed with a feeling of near hysteria.

'You have got to be joking, lady. You're social worker

to the biggest bunch of villains in London. You know that, don't you?'

At the same time he realized that he'd made a big mistake. If she was a social worker he might as well be talking to the cops, but as this thought crossed his mind, he spotted something about the way Vicky looked round the table which gave him a flicker of hope that he might still carry it off.

'Just tell me what they've done,' Vicky said sharply.

George explained.

'You must have seen it on the news,' he told her.

Vicky nodded slowly.

'I did. How do you know that they are the ones who did it?'

'I know they are,' George said, feeling anger beginning to build up inside him. 'That one,' pointing to Sonia, 'used to work in my shop till she got the sack and these two were hanging all round the shop all yesterday, and when the police get here and search this house they will find the money.'

'Supposing,' Vicky said, 'it was them. Why didn't you call the police in the first place? What do you want?'

George considered it for a moment. If this woman was who she said she was she might be trying to trap him.

'I came to make sure, before I rang the police.'

'You asked for the money,' Vicky said. She was staring with those cold eyes of hers straight into his. 'Did you have some kind of deal in mind?'

'All right,' George said. 'If they give me the money back I'll let them go.'

It suddenly occurred to him that if she agreed to the deal, she'd hardly be able to tell anyone what had happened, because she'd not only be shopping the kids, but implicating herself as well. His confidence, which had been ebbing, began to return.

Byron, who had been listening to this dialogue, and

waiting to see what would develop, thought that it was time he stuck his oar in.

'It wasn't us,' he said, 'and even if it was we don't have the money.'

By now it was clear to everyone in the room that George was after the money, rather than bursting to put them in prison.

'Let me put it this way,' George said, 'you'd better have it or you're going down.'

'We never organized all this,' Byron said. 'It was some other geezers. We just helped. They paid us all right but we only got two grand each.'

'Don't mess me about, boy,' George shouted. 'Don't mess me about.'

Juliet began to cry in earnest at the angry sound of his voice.

'Pick her up, for God's sake,' George told Sonia, moving back a couple of steps so he could keep an eye on the boys. Sonia went over and picked up Juliet, making kissing sounds and glaring indignantly at George.

'It's true,' Byron said. 'I'm not saying it was us, but you don't see the bloke that was in your house do you?'

George looked at the two of them carefully, and realized that neither of them was big enough or tall enough to be the other man he'd seen when he'd come downstairs to breakfast.

'That's right,' said Byron. 'There was two other blokes and they've got most of it. We've only got five grand between us. We put the other grand on a deposit for a flat but you can have what we've got left.'

Suddenly George's anger swept up from inside his gut like a tidal wave, blinding him, striking him dumb, and in that instant all he could do was to stick his hand out and pull the trigger. Fortunately for everyone else George aimed at the ceiling before he did so, but he had pointed in the general direction of the neon light bulb, and by some freak he'd hit it. There was a loud bang and a flash. Glass showered down from the ceiling and scattered all over the room.

'I don't give a shit,' George shouted out of this explosion. 'I want that money and you're either going to bring it right now and put it here in front of me, or I'll shoot your fucking arms off and then call the police. Don't push me, boy. I haven't forgotten that you lot broke into my house and threatened my family.'

The kitchen was half in darkness, the only light coming from the passage outside, and silhouetted against it, George was a huge, menacing and shadowed figure. In any case from the moment that he had pulled the trigger everything changed, because now they knew he was serious, or so wired that he was liable to do anything.

'I'll tell you,' Vicky shouted, her voice high and tense, in harmony with the explosive and dying echoes of the gunshot. 'They've got the money in Manchester. They were here, but they left with it on Tuesday night.'

In spite of their shock Byron and Sonia did a double-take, because it was news to them that Vicky knew any of this, and Byron shot Willie a vicious glance, as he realized how Vicky must have found out that piece of information. Vicky, in her turn, had actually swallowed Byron's story about only getting a couple of grand, and now she was setting out to convince George about the truth of what Byron said, so as to settle the whole thing.

'Give him the money you've got,' she said. 'Don't be stupid.'

'Six grand is no good to me,' George said. 'I want the lot.'

'I told you,' Byron said. 'They're in Manchester, like she said.'

'OK,' George said. 'I'll have the six grand, and then we'll talk about the rest.'

He backed out into the corridor, and shepherded them

past him into the sitting-room. When he'd got them sitting on the sofa, he put his hand in his pocket and took out an envelope which he tossed on to the coffee table in front of them. During the confusion in the kitchen he'd completely forgotten about the letter.

'Open it,' he said.

Vicky picked it up, because none of the others seemed disposed to move, and opened it.

'Read it,' George demanded.

Vicky read it aloud, her voice quavering a little. The letter was addressed to the police inspector in charge of the case, and it said how George had been suspicious of Sonia, found her, and followed her to this address where he'd recognized one of the bike boys from the previous day.

'I don't even have to phone the cops,' George said. 'If I'm not back by the morning with the money my wife is going to send a copy of that letter to the police.'

He could see that the letter worried them all. Sonia's face was stricken, and even Vicky was frowning. That lot has got them shitting themselves, George thought with satisfaction. He pointed to Vicky.

'You go and get the money.'

'I've got mine here,' Byron said hurriedly. He pulled a wad of notes out of his pocket, and slapped it down on the coffee table.

'There you are, two grand.'

In fact it was almost exactly two thousand pounds which he had in his pocket, the rest zipped securely into his duffel bag. He hoped that the others would take his cue, and only hand over two grand. What he was hoping was that George would believe their story in the end and be content with recovering six grand. Of course if that didn't work out he was prepared to fork out some more, but Byron had the sense that some kind of bargain was possible, and he wanted to start out holding as many of the cards as he could. Somehow he didn't imagine that George would want to chase the rest of the money all the way up north. The guy was a Londoner after all, and Byron guessed that a city as far away as Manchester would be too far for him to go.

Sonia gave Byron a look which told him that she understood, fumbled in the bag where she kept the baby's nappies, and the zinc cream and powder, and came up with a sheaf of notes which she put on the table beside Byron's.

'That's about two grand,' she said.

'Give him the two grand, Willie,' Byron said.

'I've got to go upstairs,' Willie told him.

'Let her go,' George pointed to Vicky again.

'In my drawer, the top one,' Willie instructed her.

He had turned away from George to speak, and he winked at her. She realized that he was trying to tell her something but for the life of her Vicky couldn't figure out what it might be. She climbed the stairs slowly, and went into Willie's room. The money was where he'd said it was, but there seemed to be a lot more than two thousand pounds. Then she realized that was why Willie had been winking at her, and she felt a surge of apprehension and anger once again. They were trying to con the man with the gun, as if they had no idea how dangerous it obviously was.

She picked up the entire bundle of money. Then it struck her that if she took it all downstairs the man would know they had been lying, and she didn't know what the consequences of that would be. As she hovered, Vicky heard the man's voice shouting up the stairs.

'Oi, up there. What you doing?'

Vicky made up her mind, and swiftly counted out two thousand pounds, shut the drawer and ran back downstairs.

'That's it, then,' George said, looking at the money in front of him. 'Now you tell me where the rest of it is.'

'She said,' Byron told him. 'It's with that lot in Manchester.'

'You'll just have to get it back then,' George said.

'You don't know,' Byron said, 'what you're on about. I don't know where they are. Don't listen to her. She don't know bugger all what she's on about. Those guys come from round Manchester, but I've got no idea where to find them.'

George sighted carefully and fired. The bullet tore across the room and buried itself in the wall above the fireplace. The effect was satisfactory. George had enjoyed pulling the trigger, and feeling the thunder in his hand, and the reaction he got was what he'd been hoping for. Sonia cringed and hugged Juliet to her. Vicky cowered away with her hands over her ears, and the expressions on the faces of Willie and Byron turned to shock and terror.

'Somebody tell him,' Vicky screamed. 'Why don't you tell him?'

Willie looked sideways at Byron.

'The next one is going right through you,' George said. He meant it too. At that moment, he knew that the battle was between him and this boy, and George was filled with a righteous certainty not only that he could win but that he deserved to, and now he had no intention of backing down from the threat he had made. Byron read all this in George's expression.

'You'll find them in Whalley Range,' he said.

The threat he perceived in George's eyes was the only thing that would have made him divulge this item, but at the back of his mind was the thought that the triplets were no pushovers, and if George thought he could hold them up and get away with it he would be getting more than he bargained for. But he hadn't counted on George working all this out for himself. Because the trouble with clever native wits like Byron, as Vicky reflected, watching the struggle of wills between him and George, was that they had huge difficulty in imagining that other people could themselves work out exactly what they were up to. The more isolated you were when you worked out how to think, the more difficult it was to understand that millions of people could use the same processes, and a lot of the time use them better.

'That's in Manchester, is it?' George asked.

Byron nodded, thinking how he would put it to the triplets when he rang them.

'All right,' George said, beginning to stuff the money into his pockets. 'We're going on a little trip.'

He gave them time to recover from the shock.

'You are going to get the rest of that money back for me,' George said, 'otherwise I swear to you you're all going to the nick.' He pointed to Byron and Sonia. 'You're coming with me, and the baby. You are going to make the deal. What I want you to do is see these geezers, get the money, bring it out and stick it in my hand. You nicked it, you're responsible. I don't give a shit. If you don't get it you're finished, mate.'

'You're mad,' Sonia said. 'Juliet should be in bed.'

'She can sleep in the car,' George said. 'I've got a daughter, remember.'

In George's mind was the idea that having Juliet and Sonia along would tie Byron's hands, and they might turn out to be useful bargaining counters. The last thing Sonia would want was to be separated from her daughter. As for the social worker, he had sussed by now that for some reason she wouldn't want to call in the police. He guessed that she was involved in some way, or else just scared about the consequences if it became public knowledge that the gang had been operating from her house, and when he thought about it and imagined what the newspapers could make out of that he could understand her reluctance. So he addressed her with some confidence.

'If I get the money back,' he said, 'you can forget all about this, like it never happened. Is that a deal?'

She nodded her head.

'It's a deal,' she said.

George suspected that sooner or later something would get out, but by then he reckoned he'd have the money tucked away, and it would be his word against theirs. Might as well be hung for a sheep as a lamb, he thought.

Chapter 19

The rush hour had ended by the time they set out, driving across Maida Vale towards Finchley Road and the M1. Byron was at the wheel. He hadn't told George about his driving licence either, and he reckoned that the one bright spot about the whole thing was that he'd get in quite a bit of practice.

George sat in the back. By now he'd put the gun away in his pocket, because he figured that he wouldn't need it unless Byron tried to turn nasty. He guessed they wouldn't try going on the run with the baby and everything. Besides, running off would be too complicated for Byron and Sonia now that he knew exactly who they were and where they were to be found. All together, George reckoned he had the situation covered, except for something he couldn't predict at all, but he was fairly certain that the robbers would prefer to give up the money rather than be arrested, and even if he had to take half, he'd still clear a good twenty grand.

It was fortunate for his own peace of mind that George had no idea that there was nearly that amount still tucked away in various corners of Vicky's house. He suspected that Byron might still be trying to con him in some way, but he had felt so much in control with the gun in his hand that the full extent of it simply did not occur to him. The roads were fast and quiet and they made good time. Of course they were still digging up some stretches of road as they always were, and there were places where they had to crawl along at thirty miles an hour, but in comparison with anything Byron had ever driven the

Volvo was smooth and fast, and he was enjoying himself as much as he could in the circumstances.

From the passenger seat Sonia kept looking back at Juliet, who had promptly fallen asleep, strapped into the portable child seat next to George, and by the time they came off the motorway at the Manchester turn-off she had her eyes closed, breathing peacefully. Byron took the Withington Road approach, and close to midnight he was pulling up down the road from the triplets' house in Whalley Range.

George gave Byron his instructions carefully. He was to go in, speak to whoever had the money, tell them what would happen if they refused to hand it over, then come out within half an hour, carrying the money. Then he was to walk up Withington Road until George picked him up. George had the suspicion that the men who had the money would already know what had happened, because he supposed that Willie would have telephoned them from London, but that didn't worry him, because if they were going to make a deal they would be ready. He wondered how Byron would justify bringing him here and the fact that he'd grassed on his mates. But he put that aspect of it out of his mind. It was Byron's problem; as long as he brought the money back, George didn't give a shit what happened in between.

Byron didn't feel the twinges of worry until he was knocking on the door of the triplets' house. By rights they should be out making their rounds, but he had a strong suspicion that Willie might have rung them, in which case they would probably be waiting. It was how they were going to react that worried him now. When he'd started out on the motorway, he hadn't been thinking about what the triplets would feel about his dropping them in it, but as he raised his hand to knock, it was the only thing on his mind.

Louis opened the door. He looked at Byron with stony

contempt, then looked past him and up and down the street.

'So where's this wanker, then?' Louis asked.

'Willie rang you?'

'Course he did,' Louis replied, his eyes still searching the street. 'Where is he, then?'

Quickly Byron told him the arrangement that George had dictated. Behind Louis he could see the other two loitering in the hallway. Suddenly Louis stepped aside and pulled Byron in, slamming the door behind him, and Byron found himself standing in the hall facing Mohammed and Ray.

'You're a fucking idiot, you know, Byron,' Mohammed said conversationally. 'If you was anybody else we'd chop your frigging head off.'

Byron felt a surge of relief. He had no idea why, but the triplets clearly didn't intend to damage him. Not seriously anyway.

'Wait a minute,' Byron said. 'I'm going to make a deal with him.'

The triplets laughed with what sounded like genuine amusement.

'We had to send our women home,' Ray said, slapping Byron lightly across the side of his head. 'You know that, don't you?'

'For God's sake,' Byron said, 'either duff me up now or let's get on with it.'

It was the sort of challenge which he knew always disarmed the triplets. Once he'd acknowledged that they could, the prospect of actually hitting him seemed to lose its charm. Mohammed grinned, looped his arm round Byron's neck, turned him round, leaned on him with all his weight and began limping into the sitting-room. The arm round his neck was uncomfortably restrictive, and Byron struggled to draw breath as Mohammed's forearm squeezed his windpipe painfully. But Byron knew better than to protest and when they reached the sofa Mohammed let him go without any more fuss and sat down, stretching his bad leg out in front, and tapping the shoe gently with his stick.

'What you got in mind, then?'

'I figure,' Byron said, 'that this geezer will shut up and go away if he gets enough of the money. He's already got our money back, fifteen grand, and I reckon if you kick him another ten he'll just piss off and leave us alone.'

'Ten grand,' Mohammed said thoughtfully. He drew in his breath through his teeth and shook his head regretfully. 'Ten grand out of pocket. Byron, Byron, Byron. That's a lot of money, and we got no guarantee.'

'He can't exactly go to the cops, can he?'

'I don't know what he's got in mind,' Mohammed said in a tone of deep worry, although the smile on his face contradicted his tone. 'Faith is a fine invention,' Mohammed continued, 'when gentlemen can see, but microscopes are prudent in an emergency.'

Byron knew Mohammed was winding him up, especially when he started quoting poetry, but he gave no sign, merely waited for something to come out of the triplets' collective mind.

'Suppose,' Mohammed said, 'we said you had to compensate us.'

'It would take time,' Byron told him. 'I'm bloody broke.'

The triplets laughed in unison.

'Leave off telling us lies,' Mohammed said. 'Don't tell me none of that money didn't stick to your little fingers, boy. 'Cause if it didn't you haven't half changed since we were kids. We'll hand this wally that money if you personally guarantee to pay it back within a month.'

Byron considered the problem. From the triplets' point of view it was a reasonable way to do business. If things went wrong they couldn't make a claim for the insurance.

Somebody had to be responsible for the debt, and it was him. But if he said yes he'd have absolutely nothing left and he'd have to start again. Next time things might turn out worse, and he didn't think he could face setting up another scam so soon after this one had gone so definitely wrong.

'Come on, boys,' he said. 'You know I'd be a complete idiot to agree. I'm deep in the shit as it is.' He spread his hands in appeal. 'Come on, boys. All for one and one for all. What we gonna do?'

Mohammed's expression didn't change. He stared at Byron steadily, his eyes boring straight into his, and without looking Byron knew that Louis and Ray were staring at him in exactly the same fixed manner. Suddenly Mohammed's eyes widened, and a stifled sound emerged from his lips. Byron wasn't at that moment sure whether this was an explosion of rage and his muscles tensed, but behind him he heard Ray start to giggle and instantaneously the triplets were all roaring with laughter, Louis beating his fists up and down on the arm of the sofa, unable to control his mirth.

'We were only joking, you wally,' Mohammed said. 'We're not going to give this git back a shit. Do leave off. As hell as like.'

Suddenly Byron remembered the letter, and he told Mohammed about it and what it said.

'Does it say anything about us?' Mohammed said.

Byron thought furiously. He would have liked to say yes, but there was no way he could explain how George would have known about the triplets before he got to the house, and in any case he wouldn't have known what their names were, or what they looked like, or even the fact that they were triplets.

'So,' Mohammed summarized. 'He don't know nothing about us then, and there's nothing about us in that letter anyway.'

Byron nodded reluctantly.

'Well, right then,' Mohammed said. 'What you lot do if anything happens is move out that house, and if they can be bothered tracking you down, just tell them bloody lies. They got no proof. Can't do you without no proof. Anyone seen you was looking at a masked man. Might as well be the fucking Lone Ranger as far as they know. Just forget about that letter shit.'

'What are we supposed to do then?' Byron asked.

'Let's bargain,' Mohammed said. 'Tell him we'll give him same as you. Six grand. See what he says. If he doesn't like it we'll make him another offer.'

'He's got Sonia and the baby in the car,' Byron said.

'Tell him to send her with the next offer then,' Mohammed said. He chuckled. 'You can hang about with this nutcase pointing a gun at your head, Byron. If you're that bothered.'

Around him the triplets chuckled at Mohammed's humour.

'What you waiting for?' Louis said. 'Your half hour's up.'

'What happens if he turns the next offer down?'

'Ah,' Ray said, flicking at his chin with his fingers, doing his Robert de Niro impersonation. 'We make him an offer he don' refuse.'

'Go,' Louis muttered impatiently. 'Go.'

Byron went. He walked slowly up Withington Road, wondering what would happen next, where George and Sonia and the baby were, and what plan the triplets were cooking up.

At the same time George was driving down Oxford Road from the city centre. They were late, but he guessed that he'd be catching up with Byron before he'd had a chance to walk more than a few blocks. They had gone driving through the city centre, and George had stopped to buy a takeaway of duck and fried noodles in Chinatown. Afterwards he'd parked in St Peter's Square opposite the library, and eaten the lot. Sonia, who had refused to join him, had watched him impassively all the time.

'You don't have any idea,' she said suddenly, 'what you're doing. Those guys can kill you, and if you get on their nerves they probably will.'

George smiled. He'd been in the business before it had become a collar and tie adjunct of big city stockbroking, and he'd more than once come across some of the men who came out of the most vicious East End gangs. He knew that a killer looked like, because he'd shaken hands and shared a drink with some of them. He could well believe that young darkies like the ones who had robbed him could kill if they got in a fight or their blood was up, but having sat in the car for four hours with Byron, he knew that he was not the sort of nutter who could knock someone off casually.

'I'm not talking about Byron,' Sonia said, as if she'd been reading his mind. 'The guys who you sent him to see about the money are really bad, believe me.'

George was struck by her obvious sincerity, and he remembered vaguely reading in the Sunday paper about the gangs in Moss Side and witnesses being intimidated and shot. But that was different, he reminded himself. Real hard men were like the Axe Man or Mad Jack, or some of them geezers who would make no bones about taking on a squad of security men with a pickaxe handle. He knew what violent men were like, George thought, and so far he'd not seen anything he couldn't handle.

'All right,' he said, humouring her. 'What would you do if you were me?'

'I'd pack it in,' Sonia replied, 'and cut my losses, and piss off home while I still could.'

George gave her a short bark of sarcastic laughter.

'That would suit you and your mates. Wouldn't it? Give you a bloody good laugh.'

'That's not why I'm saying it,' Sonia said, which was true, because for the last hour or so, even though George had terrified her, and was making life awkward, it occasionally crossed her mind how fond she'd once been of him, and how badly he must feel about the way they'd held him up and terrified his wife and child.

'Thanks for the advice,' George said, carefully throwing the foil containers which held the remains of his noodles at a bin stuck on the lamppost near the car. He missed, but he didn't notice because he was already looking at his watch to see whether it was time to go and find Byron.

Withington Road was deserted, except for a small group of young men and women, who had the haggard and shaggy look of left-wing students, lounging outside the kebab shop. A couple of turnings further on George caught sight of Byron. He slowed down and stopped. He wound the window down and Byron came round and leaned on it.

'Where's the money?' George asked.

'They wouldn't go for it,' Byron said. 'They're willing to go to six grand.'

'Forget it,' George said. 'You're going back to the nick. And your young mate, you'd better get him a rubber implant up his arsehole. They like nice young lads like that where he's going.'

'Leave off,' Byron said. 'I think they'll forward a bit more, but you've got to be reasonable.' He was pleading.

'What's reasonable?'

'Get what you can,' Byron said. 'We can scrape up another couple of grand back in London. Maybe I can get Vicky to kick in something. You've got six, if they give you eight maybe we can make it up to seventeen or eighteen.'

'You got away with forty grand,' George said. 'That's what I want.'

Beside him Sonia shifted, and looked over at Byron. Cunning bastard, she thought. Byron noted her reaction, but he had too much on his plate right then to worry about it.

'No chance,' he told George. 'Why don't you just take what you can get?'

George thought for a minute.

'You've got this money in the house in London?' he asked.

'Yes.'

George smiled. He'd had the feeling that this toe-rag was hiding something.

'Twenty grand,' he said. 'Can you make it up to twenty grand?'

'Yes.'

The admission was being wrung out of Byron, but he guessed that if it would get them all out of this without any more trouble it was worth it. He could pay off George and he'd still have a few bob stashed.

'All right,' George said. 'You see what you can get, then we go on back to London and get the rest.'

Byron heaved a sigh of relief. If he could persuade the triplets, the final deal would merely be a question of everyone getting a smaller share. All wouldn't be lost, and the next time they did anything like this he'd be a lot more careful. Of course he had been careful enough, it was simply the fact that this mad bastard had figured out about Sonia, which Byron supposed he really should have foreseen.

Back at the house Mohammed opened the door. Byron looked around automatically for Louis and Ray, but they didn't seem to be there.

'Where's the boys?' Byron asked.

‘They’re out doing the business,’ Mohammed said airily.

Byron suspected that this was a lie, but there was nothing he could do about it, so he launched straight into telling Mohammed about the arrangement he’d made with George. He left out the bit about there being more money back in London but assured them that George would accept it if they gave him eight.

‘Doesn’t matter, Byron,’ Mohammed said immediately. ‘Eight grand’s nothing to us, man. We only did it to help you out.’

He handed Byron a bag.

‘Open it.’

Byron opened it. The bag was full of notes strapped together in bundles with rubber bands.

‘Give it to him,’ Mohammed said, ‘and tell him don’t show his face round here again.’

Byron said goodbye, and walked off up Withington Road, feeling as if he’d won the pools or something. It had been a tricky situation, but he’d managed to get them out of it. Tomorrow, he thought, as soon as they got back, and paid off George, he would split with his share of the loot. After that no one would find him. It had been bad luck, sticking around with Sonia and her baby and Willie too. On his own he could travel fast, and travel light, and from now on that was what he was going to do.

When George pulled up beside him again, Byron got into the car without hesitation.

‘This is it,’ he told George handing him the bag. ‘They won’t go any further.’

George contemplated, for a moment, going up to the house where he’d dropped off Byron, and forcing them to cough up the rest, but he had the sense, especially after what Sonia had told him, that it would be a stupid move, and he calculated that twenty grand would just about see him right, in any case. Of course he'd have preferred to have had the whole lot, but sometimes, he told himself, half a loaf was better than no bread.

He got out and changed seats with Byron, going back to his place behind the driver, and they took off, following the signs towards the motorway back down south to London. Sonia, who by now was worn out, leaned against the window and fell asleep. George was too keyed up to sleep, and anyway he had to stay awake in order to keep an eye on Byron, but his mind was tuned so tightly to the issue of the money and collecting it when they got back that he felt he was in a sort of dream, slashing through the night as if he was speeding along some dark tunnel in his own mind. Byron was busy calculating the figures, wondering whether Sonia had interpreted what she'd heard correctly, and thinking up different ways of stopping her from demanding a larger share. So everyone in the car was too preoccupied to notice the headlights behind, or if they did, they failed to attach any meaning to them.

They were well out of the city, and just arrived at the junction bordering the cemetery gates, when another car cut in front of them and stopped abruptly at the red light. Byron pulled up behind him, then looking ahead felt a tendril of recognition fingering his tired brain. But before it could flower into knowledge he felt a draught of cold air on the back of his neck. He looked round, knowing what had happened before he saw the tall figure, hat pulled down over his forehead, dark glasses, coat collar pulled up to hide his face. He had opened the door next to George, and was holding a pistol with what looked like an abnormally long barrel against the bookie's temple.

'Everybody out,' Louis said. George got out slowly, and Louis pushed him to the other side of the car by the pavement.

In the meantime Ray, dressed in the same fashion, had got out of the car in front and come back. He reached in the back of the Volvo, and took out the bag Byron had given George. Then he calmly tossed it into the boot of his own car. Byron shook Sonia awake, and she unstrapped Juliet and got out on to the pavement, looking around sleepily and pressing Juliet's head down on her bosom.

'Go and sit in that car behind,' Ray said.

Sonia went without a word, but Byron loitered on the pavement. He had a horrible feeling that the brothers were about to do something terrible, and he was torn between the impulse to interfere, and the sense that if he did, they would almost certainly turn on him.

'Touch me,' George told them, looking straight into the dark glasses, 'and the lot of you are in the shit.'

'Yeah. We heard,' Louis said, and hit George hard with an underarm right hand straight into the lower stomach. George bent over, buckling at the knees, his breath rushing out of his lungs in a long rattling gasp. Louis held him under the arms and straightened him up against the car.

'Listen good, chum,' Louis said in a quiet and intense voice. 'We don't give a shit about your letter, or about who you tell, and what you tell them. We've got alibis up to here, you stupid fucker.'

Ray put his arm round George's neck, choking his wind off, and bent his right arm up behind his back. George's face went mauve as the air was cut off, and his mouth opened in the desperate effort to breathe. At the same time Louis raised the gun and pushed the barrel right into his mouth.

'Say good bye, sucker,' Louis said.

Watching them, Byron saw what was happening too late to interfere effectively, but when he heard what Louis said he jumped forward, some mad thought in his head of pulling Louis's arm down. All he could think was – no, no, no, and all the time he knew that he would be too late. And he would have been, except that instead of the expected roar of the shot he heard a loud click. Louis turned and looked at Byron. Byron stopped. Louis smiled. He took the gun out of George's mouth and put it in his pocket. Ray let George go, and the bookie leant against the car clutching at his stomach, and drawing great breaths of air into his lungs, with a whooping, crying sound.

'Look at that,' Louis said in a disgusted tone. 'You've only gone and pissed yourself.'

At the front of George's trousers there was a huge spreading stain.

'Charming,' Ray said.

'You see how easy it is,' Louis told George, holding his chin between his thumb and fingers and staring into his eyes. 'We know where you live. We can find you any time, and even if we were banged up our mates can find you. You know exactly how that goes. Then there's your wife and your daughter. You know what I mean?'

George nodded feebly.

'All right then,' Louis said. 'Just stop fucking about. Forget about writing letters. Go home and relax, and think about what might happen if we get pissed off.'

Louis turned to Ray.

'Give us a grand out that bag.'

Ray went over to his car, opened the boot, fiddled in the back and came back. He handed Louis one of the bundles of notes, and Louis tucked it into the inside pocket of George's jacket.

'Here, that's for you,' he said. 'So you didn't waste your trip up here.'

He patted George kindly on the cheek, and turned casually to walk back to his car, then changed his mind, took a knife out of his pocket, opened it, bent down, and plunged it into each of the rear tyres on the Volvo. Then he straightened up, folded his knife, put it in his pocket, and walked past Byron.

'Don't just stand there, Byron,' he said. 'Let's go.'

Chapter 20

They drove away calmly, Louis making a U-turn after the lights, and driving straight back down the way they had come. Byron avoided looking at him. Sonia was sitting in the back cuddling Juliet, her eyes downcast, her mouth pursed as if she was trying to subtract herself from what was going on round her.

'Why didn't you tell me?' Byron asked.

'We didn't want to worry you,' Louis said, smiling. Byron made a sound of disgust and Louis's smile grew wider.

'Don't worry,' Louis said. 'You're all right now I tell you. That geezer won't bother you any more.'

Byron wasn't so sure, and he intended vanishing as he had planned as soon as he got back to London and collected his money. Then it struck him that they ought to be on their way.

'How you getting back?' Louis asked.

Byron thought wildly. It was after two o'clock and there'd be no trains.

'Bugger it,' he said.

Louis laughed.

'Don't worry,' he said. 'We thought of that.'

In a few minutes they were back in front of the house. They went in so that Sonia could go to the toilet. Byron wanted to go too, and Louis said he would do them a cup of tea and a sandwich before they left. Byron still didn't know what they had in mind, because Louis wouldn't tell him, and every time he asked, the triplets had a mass giggle, which worried Byron more than the thought of how they were getting back.

'Don't worry,' Mohammed said. 'It won't be no trouble. What it is, we've got this car down the road. Nice one too. We'll go and get it in a minute.'

They left Juliet and Sonia on the sitting-room sofa, and walked up the road towards Moss Lane, Mohammed limping with a jaunty vigour. The other boys had tried to get him to sit still but he said he'd been sitting round all night and now he wanted to see the fun. After a few minutes it struck Byron that there was something familiar about the route they were taking and he wasn't too surprised when they came in sight of the tower block where Marie lived with Hyacinth and Fergus. What surprised him was to see the red Renault on top of which he'd fallen, the roof caved in, and the windscreen out, still pulled up by the side of the road, its interior now looted, the doors sagging open and the wheels vanished.

'It only took one night,' Louis said, 'for them youths to finish that car off. You started it. Fucking vandal.'

The triplets laughed, and Ray cuffed Byron lightly across the back of his head. Byron wished he'd stop doing that.

'Where are we going then?'

'We're there,' Louis said. He pointed to a gleaming black BMW which stood at a short distance away.

'That's it,' Louis announced.

Byron looked at him suspiciously.

'This is the car you're going to lend me?' he asked.

'That's right,' Louis said. 'Don't say we don't look after you. This car belongs to Fergus. We reckoned we might burn it, just for a bit of fun like, but makes more sense being constructive. You can get back down to London in style driving this, man.'

'What about Fergus?' Byron said.

'Don't worry about him, man,' Ray told him. 'He's in

bed now, and he never gets up till gone lunchtime.' He clicked his tongue self-righteously. 'I don't know. Nobody ever told him the early bird gets the worm. By the time he notices his motor's gone you'll have got rid of it.'

Mohammed already had the door of the car open and they got in, and Mohammed drove them steadily back down Moss Lane, the brothers stroking the interior of the car and admiring its finish.

'What you do,' Louis said, 'is drop it somewhere, Brixton like or Hackney, leave it unlocked, I mean crack the door open a little, make it obvious you know. By the time you're home some kid will have nicked it, and then God knows where it will end up, but it won't be down to you. You got that?'

He nudged Byron, and Byron nodded.

'What about Fergus?' he asked again. The triplets roared with laughter.

'What a laugh we'll have,' Mohammed said, 'watching him belting round trying to decide if he can afford to call in the police and trying to sort out which youth had the guts to nick his motor.'

Byron understood at last that it was one of the triplets' little jokes, which combined settling a score and enjoying someone else's discomfort. Privately he reckoned that this time he'd had enough of the triplets and after this he would know better than to get in touch with them again.

They parked nearly half a street up from the house. Mohammed and Ray walked down the road to get Sonia and Juliet, while Louis stayed with Byron to keep him company.

'Why don't you come back up here?' Louis asked Byron. 'It would be like the old days.'

It struck Byron that none of this seemed at all weird to the triplets, because it was simply like an advanced version of the sort of thing they'd been doing while they were kids.

'I want to make a fresh start,' Byron told him. 'What I want to do is look around a bit, check things out and start working out what I want to do with my life.'

Louis nodded sagely, as if he understood what that was all about. Suddenly a puzzled expression crossed his face and he put his hand on Byron's arm, squeezing it painfully, but when Byron looked round he was gazing into space as if unaware of what he was doing.

'Something's wrong,' Louis said.

Before Byron could react, Louis had thrown open the door of the BMW and was running up towards his house. Byron got out, looked after him, and followed reluctantly. He didn't want to be involved in anything else that the triplets were doing that night, but he couldn't just leave Sonia and Juliet. Once again he swore to himself that if he got out of this alive he would never speak to the triplets again if he could help it.

As it happened, if they'd approached the house by a different route they would have seen George's Volvo parked at a crazy angle to the pavement. This would have surprised Louis anyway, because he hadn't given George another thought, and in his own mind at any rate, he was quite satisfied that they had finished with the bookie. But George wasn't finished with him.

At the moment that Louis had walked off, leaving him alone by the side of the road with two flat tyres, the bookie felt that he'd had hit rock bottom. But Louis, in his confidence, had gone too far. It hadn't even occurred to either him or Ray that George could give them any trouble and they hadn't, for instance, searched for his gun or bothered themselves about it. But their contempt for him wasn't what was hurting George. He could have coped with being threatened, and having now encountered these guys he knew that they were serious, and, in most circumstances he would have then left them strictly alone, not being stark staring mad. But Louis had humiliated him to the last inch of his being. Every time he felt the damp down his legs it reminded him of that blinding moment when all the sensations in the world had rushed through him, and every one of his senses stopped dead waiting for the gun to roar, and his bladder had opened, although he didn't know it at the time, so that all he'd felt was this warm rush flooding through his brain like the climax of a wet dream.

George walked round, still holding on to the body of the car, and looked at the two flat tyres. After all that, he thought, the bastard had been vicious enough to puncture his tyres, and it was that final petty gesture which decided him. He thought of Rhona, but only for the merest fraction of a second, and then what he thought was that he couldn't go back to her feeling like this, and a kind of rage flooded through him, driving out all the other emotions. He squatted down, and patiently changed one of the tyres. As he did this he kept looking round, eyeing the passing cars. There had to be a phone booth somewhere around, but when he thought of the time that the AA would take to get there he rejected the idea of calling them. His only thought was to get back at the men who'd done this to him, and he could not endure the thought of waiting any longer than he had to. He had just finished tightening the nuts when another car drew up at the lights. Several cars had already passed, but this was the right model. The same Volvo as his. Of course it was a popular make, but he still saw it as a stroke of luck which confirmed his determination.

George went across and rapped on the passenger window. The man driving was balding and middle-aged. Some sort of salesman, George guessed, from the jacket carefully hung on a hanger and dangling in the back. He looked round when George knocked, hesitated for a moment, then slid the window open a couple of inches.

'I need a spare tyre,' George said urgently. 'I'll give you two hundred and fifty quid for yours.'

In the end he had to pay the man another hundred more than he'd offered, but George thought it was money well spent, and within another quarter of an hour he was driving back into Moss Side. When he got there, he simply walked up to the door, knocked on it, and luck being what it was, Sonia, alone in the house with Juliet, answered the door, her mouth dropping open immediately in a scream of terror and surprise at the sight of George standing on the doorstep, the gun in his hand extended so that she was looking cross-eyed at the tip of the barrel.

George pushed her roughly back along the hallway. He had a sudden sense that he had done this before, and somewhere in his mind the memory of holding up Vicky in the same way bubbled up and crossed with what was happening.

'They're out,' Sonia squeaked. 'I'm the only one here.'

When Mohammed and Ray arrived they didn't notice anything unusual, and it was only when they came into the sitting-room, and Mohammed had plonked himself down in the armchair while Ray went to pick up Juliet, that George slammed the door, put his back to it, and pointed the gun at them.

'All right, you fuckers, I'll take that money now,' George said.

The brothers froze with astonishment.

'Who the fuck are you?' Mohammed said, although, as George realized, he knew precisely.

'No games,' George said. He felt very tired. His body was like a rag held together standing straight by the simple force of his will. The patch on his trousers was nearly dry, but he knew that he smelled, the stink of his urine wafting round him in recurring waves.

Mohammed took in the look of him, guessing that Louis had pushed the man over some sort of edge and that instead of being broken the way most people were, George had found some dangerous engine of obsession to drive him back here with the gun in his hand. Mohammed held his hands up in a gesture of surrender.

'Let's talk about this,' he said ingratiatingly. 'I never knew what these bastards did. As far as I'm concerned you can have the money back. No trouble. But I mean let's discuss it.'

'I said no games,' George said, unimpressed. 'The money is what I want.'

'Give it to him,' Mohammed said.

Ray moved cautiously over to the side of the room, George's gun following him carefully as he went, picked up the bag he'd brought in earlier and held it out.

'And the rest of it,' George said.

Mohammed looked at him, considering. He guessed that George had expended a massive burst of energy in simply getting here, and he estimated if he kept him talking long enough, he would either fold up and agree to a compromise, or collapse all together.

'That's about it,' Mohammed said.

'No games,' George shouted. 'I've had enough. Money, money, money. You fucking find it or you're dead.'

He didn't know any more what he was saying. All he knew was that he had to get his own back. He had to squeeze these bastards, and he would make them pay for everything he felt if he had to go through every inch of the house and take everything they'd got.

'Fuck off,' Mohammed said briefly, and sat down.

In reply, and without hesitation, George shot him, the gun exploding with a sort of spanging roar like some strange clash of hammer on metal. Mohammed screamed, jerked convulsively off the chair and fell over on the floor. For a moment the room stood still, everyone gripped by the same sensation of shock and surprise, not least George, who hadn't known that he was going to pull the trigger until it happened. Ray was the one who recovered first. As Mohammed writhed on the floor Ray screamed, a weird high-pitched sound coming out of his bull-like chest. At the same time he was answered by a roar from the hallway as Louis came charging in, already shouting, in answer to Mohammed's cry of pain. Caught between two fires George hesitated, the gun wavering towards the door, then back again towards Ray, who in the meantime had reached for the nearest thing to hand, which happened to be the triplets' souvenir cabinet. Five foot high, glass and all, he picked it up, heaved it smoothly, no effort at all, and with what seemed like superhuman strength hammered it straight over George's head, as if trying to drive him into the ground like a nail.

The gun went off again, and George went down under the cabinet, jerked for one instant like a fish trying to escape the net, and then lay still. Both Ray and Louis ignored him, leaping to Mohammed's side and raising him between them like one of those pictures, Sonia thought, of a hero wounded on the battlefield. By now Juliet, who had come awake with a convulsive grabbing of her hands when she heard the shot, was sitting up in Sonia's arms screaming without a moment's pause in between, like some inhuman machine for noise-making.

'Take her outside, you stupid cow,' Ray shouted. 'There's milk in the kitchen.'

Sonia got up and went hurriedly out into the hallway and through to the kitchen. As she went, Byron came in through the outer door and slammed it shut. But she ignored him, even though he called out to her.

Byron shrugged, and walked on down to the sitting-room door, but the sight that greeted him when he got there was like a fulfilment of one of his nightmares. There was blood all over the place, on the furniture, on the floor, and a diagonal line of spots crossing one wall like a row of plaster ducks. As he took all this in, the brothers came towards him, carrying Mohammed, his shirt soaked in blood, his eyes closed.

'Is he?' Byron heard himself saying the stupid phrase, but he couldn't bring himself to say the next word.

'He'll be all right,' Louis said, without pausing. 'You'd best piss off.'

Byron went a little way into the sitting-room to look at George. He shifted the cabinet, and it slid off George's body with a thump and a rattle. Byron saw then that his hands were wet, slick and dripping with blood. When he'd moved the cabinet, blood had splashed everywhere. He'd knelt down to look, and the damp feeling along his knees and trouser legs was George's blood. The bookie's head lolled sideways at an impossible angle, and as Byron reached out to touch him he realized that there was a long, bloody splinter of glass shaped like a knife blade sticking out of his neck. Byron got up and backed cautiously towards the door as if he expected George to move. As he went a long trickle of blood flowed from the body towards him, and he stepped backwards hurriedly through the door, closing it in front of him, as if closing a curtain or pressing a switch which would blank out the images inside the room for ever.

Chapter 21

There was no hurry now, and Byron drove the BMW at a steady speed down the motorway back to London. Before he left he had changed his clothes, borrowing a pair of the triplets' jeans and a T-shirt and a pair of sneakers. All of them were too big for him but he reckoned that was better than driving down the motorway covered in blood at the wheel of a stolen car. It had crossed his mind to take the bag full of money, but thinking about the triplets' reaction, he suppressed the idea immediately. Sonia seemed to have retreated completely into herself, saying nothing at all as she climbed in cuddling Juliet, who by now had stopped screaming her head off, but still cried steadily for the first hour or so on the road. When Byron looked round, he saw that Sonia was crying too, but there was nothing he could say, because he felt like crying himself.

It was near dawn, gone six o'clock, when they drove into London, the lights of the city turning the night into day as they went. Byron took Louis's hint, and dropped the car near one of the estates in Neasden. Then they walked to the main road and got a cab from the minicab office. They got out on the corner and walked slowly towards the house. Byron was thinking about breakfast. He had nearly stopped at one of the motorway caffs, but somehow it seemed he would be taking too much of a risk and in the end he thought it best to get rid of the car before doing anything else.

On the way Byron told Sonia that they would have to

leave as soon as they'd had something to eat and sorted themselves out.

'Where are we going?' Sonia said.

She said it lifelessly, as if she had lost her own will and was depending on him to tell her; and thinking about it, Byron wasn't at all surprised that she should be reacting like this. The trouble was that he had intended to go off on his own, but if George had been telling the truth about his letter there'd probably be some sort of investigation, and they'd be looking for Sonia. If they found her, he didn't know what would happen. On the other hand, he was sure that if they went away and kept themselves quiet for a bit things would blow over. After all, what would the cops have? George's suspicion of Sonia, that was all; they might want to question her, but if they couldn't find her for a while they would forget about it. She could change her name. Perhaps they could go abroad. But he couldn't afford to leave her on her own in her present state. That was certain. He was certain too, that George and his car would disappear without a trace somewhere up north. It will all blow over, Byron told himself.

'I don't know,' he told Sonia. 'Maybe we'll piss off to the seaside. What do you reckon?'

She didn't reply, but he guessed that meant she didn't mind.

The house was dark and silent. Sonia went upstairs to put Juliet to bed, so she could have a rest while they sorted out what to do. Byron went on into the kitchen, moving quietly so as not to disturb Vicky and Willie. He'd have to say something to them in a minute. It was all right for them, he thought. Whatever happened Vicky could say that they'd simply been in the house and she didn't know what they were up to, and she'd probably be believed. That was how it was if you were someone like her.

He didn't see the letter until he had put the kettle on, and sat down again. Then he noticed the long white envelope lying in the middle of the table with his name printed on it. Frowning, he picked it up. This was probably Vicky handing out the order for them to go immediately, and Byron's lips twisted in a sneer as he ripped it open. Another envelope fell out, but he shook open the sheets of paper in which it was wrapped to see what it was all about. What he read right away made him slam the letter down unbelievingly. At the same time he heard Sonia running down the stairs and along the corridor. She threw the door open so that it flew back and banged against the wall.

'Me money's gone,' Sonia said. 'Vicky and Willie have gone and all. What's going on?'

Byron stared at her for a moment then leapt up and, pushing out past her, ran to the stairs, fell on his knees and began ripping up the stair carpet. There was nothing there. He'd secreted about twelve grand in the end, and all of it had vanished. Willie. He'd never have thought it. It must be Vicky. He rushed back into the kitchen where Sonia was reading the letter, every line of her face and body uttering shock and disbelief.

Their reaction wouldn't have surprised Vicky, because when she'd written the letter she had an inkling of how the two friends would receive it, but by this time she had hardened her heart against them and, as she said to Willie, she couldn't care less. The most difficult part, of course, had been persuading Willie. The truth was that when she'd heard what they had done, and realized that she couldn't go to the police, Vicky had felt a wave of anger and disgust so strong that it almost overpowered her. After George had marched Byron and Sonia out of the door she sat trembling, her mind in a turmoil. Whatever happened, she thought, she was now involved.

Unless she could put Willie in prison, and she was sure that was what would happen if she went to the law, she would have to think of some other way of sorting out the situation. In that moment she nearly picked up the phone to call Jill, but immediately understood how stupid that would be. But it wasn't until she heard Willie talking on the telephone to Manchester that she realized what she would have to do.

When Willie put the phone down she took his hand, drew him into the study and made him sit down. She told him the options quickly and brutally.

'We have to go away for a bit,' she told Willie. Poor innocent, she thought, as she saw the look of astonishment cross his face. She explained. Whatever happened, she intended to extricate him from the situation. His friends wouldn't leave him out of it, she said. He had begun to live a normal life until Byron came along, and she didn't believe that now all this had happened Willie could simply go on as he had before. She reminded him about what Byron had done to her, just in order to stay in the house for a few days. What would he do next?

'Nothing,' Willie said weakly. 'It's all over now.'

She looked Willie in the eye, exerting the full force of her will.

'Do you really believe that, Willie?' she asked.

Willie looked away eventually, and shook his head.

'All right,' Vicky said, 'let me tell you the bottom line. I'm going away. I want you to come with me, but if you won't it's all over for you here. You'll have to move out now, and I don't want to see you again when I come back.'

Saying this, Vicky felt a sense of freedom and decision. Now she knew that what had been wrong all along was the fact that she'd been letting things happen to her, without being able to take control one way or the other, and that habit was somehow tied up with her job and her constipated way of life. Doing this would break all the chains of the careful rules she lived by. Whatever happens, she thought, it'll be different.

Watching Vicky and taking in what she was threatening, Willie thought for a moment about Byron and Sonia and being El Segundo, and the times they'd spent together late at night talking about their mums and about the way that Sonia had kissed him and touched him. Then he thought about being on his own without Vicky to look after him, and searching around for somewhere to live, and being sat at the kitchen table telling Vicky about his day.

'All right,' Willie said. 'What do you want us to do?'

'I want to get on the ferry,' Vicky said, 'and wake up tomorrow in a hotel in Paris. Then we can have breakfast, look around the city, you'll love it, have a wonderful lunch, then start driving across the country to Spain. We might end up in Portugal, or we might take a plane and go to the Caribbean, sit on a beach for a while. How about that?'

Willie grinned.

'All right,' he said simply.

Vicky wrote the letters during the next half hour. One to her office, resigning, and asking for immediate leave without pay owing to a bereavement. Another to her friend Jill, and the last one to Byron and Sonia. When she'd finished she collected the money which was scattered all over the house. She had known about Byron's stash the morning after he'd put the notes under the carpet. After all, this was her house in which she'd lived for so many years, and she noticed even the tiniest changes. She hadn't touched the money till then, meaning to confront Byron about it before he left. Now she collected all of it, and zipped it neatly into a small travelling bag. At the last moment she relented, and counted out a thousand pounds which she sealed in a smaller envelope and stuck into Byron's letter.

'They'll be able to manage on that,' she told Willie.

'What about your bills and that?' Willie asked. He was already beginning to think of himself as a responsible part of their partnership. Hearing the serious note in his voice, Vicky smiled fondly and explained about standing orders.

'Jill will take care of the rest.'

They set out almost immediately, and made the late-night ferry at Folkestone, so by the time Byron and Sonia were reading the letter which told them their doom, Vicky and Willie had just checked in to a hotel on the Left Bank, and Vicky was calling room service to order a breakfast of coffee and croissants. As she did so she wondered for a second whether Byron and Sonia had got back and found the letter yet, but she put the thought out of her head immediately, and when she put the phone down, she looked over and grinned at Willie, thinking about how they would spend the rest of the day.

At exactly the same time as Vicky and Willie were tucking into their breakfast, Byron and Sonia were just beginning to take in what had happened.

'By the time you read this letter,' they read, holding the letter between them, Sonia's hand shaking so violently that they had to rest it on the table and sit down to finish reading, 'Willie and I will be abroad. I am sure you will understand our reasons for leaving, and I advise you both to get out of the house as quickly as possible. I've arranged to have the locks changed at lunchtime, and I would suggest that you leave by then, if not sooner. Please do not feel that Willie is being disloyal to your friendship. He has his whole life ahead of him, and the most important thing for him to do now is to keep out of the sort of trouble that you are doing your best to involve him in. I hope you don't feel too upset about the money. I've left you more than enough to set yourselves up somewhere and make a fresh start, which I strongly advise you to do. You should have learnt one thing, and that is that if you can't be trusted yourself, then you can't trust anyone else either. You are sharp and clever, and you ought to put those qualities to better use. What you are doing now won't help you at all in the long run, and I'm sure you understand that what you must resolve for yourself is what to do about it. Best of luck. I hope everything turned out well. Vicky.'

Byron sat still for several moments, reading the letter over and over again. Sonia had burst into tears, but he paid no attention, his mind locked on to the thought of Vicky and Willie speeding through the countryside, looking at each other with affection and laughing. He had expected the emotion he felt to be pure hatred, but what was inside him was a sense of loss, and he understood that in some peculiar way he had wanted to be part of the bond between the two of them, but all he could do to make that happen was to attack it.

'What should we do now?' Sonia wailed. She was looking round fearfully, as if expecting the police to burst in at any moment.

Byron got up from the table, folding the letter carefully and tucking it away into his pocket. He didn't know it then but he would keep it until it fell apart, reading it over and over again. He opened the envelope with the money, counted it and put that in his pocket too. He looked at Sonia, wondering what to do about her. All this was her fault. Then he thought that she was all he had left from the old days, and it crossed his mind that he would be feeling a lot worse if she hadn't been there.

'I'll call a taxi,' he said. 'You get Juliet and pack your stuff up. We're going to Brighton.'